Praise for

Joe Pernice

"When I think of Joe's music there's a sort of emotional or ethereal quality to it. . . . I had an image of him as a delicate sensibility. But the book is so comically hard-boiled. There's this willingness to be funny in a crude but verbally dexterous way." —Tom Perotta, *Los Angeles Times*

"Unexpectedly touching . . . Talking 'bout his generation, Pernice is in his element. The narrative is built on quips and quirky metaphors, ending with a poignant image of the quixotic slacker." —*The Boston Globe*

"Deftly conjured . . . *It Feels So Good When I Stop* is consistently readable, tight, occasionally very funny, always in key and endearing to the degree that it knows just when to stop." —*San Francisco Chronicle*

"Terrific . . . complete with broken hearts, empty bottles, and a deep obsession with music." —*The Portland Mercury*

"Reading indie pop musician Joe Pernice's debut novel, *It Feels So Good When I Stop*, is like being assaulted by Charles Bukowski after listening to Dusty Springfield." —*New York Post*

"Funny and sharply observed." —*Magnet*

"The novel is a real kick: a dark-toned work with moments of great humor and relish, thanks to a lovably screwed-up narrator who strikes much the same world-weary, sophisticated tone as found in many of Pernice's best songs."

—*The Patriot Ledger*

"Observed with impeccable clarity, *It Feels So Good When I Stop* is a very funny, profoundly human novel, perfectly attuned to the quotidian grotesque of twenty-first-century America." —William Gibson, author of *Spook Country*

"One can accept, reluctantly, Pernice's apparently inexhaustible ability to knock out brilliant three-minute pop songs—just about any Pernice Brothers record contains half a dozen tunes comparable to Elvis Costello's best work. But now it turns out he can write fiction too, and so envy and bitterness become unavoidable."

—Nick Hornby, *The Believer*

"Quite a remarkable piece of writing. Acidic, profane, and easily one of the most lethal and unrelentingly hilarious books that I have ever read."

—Jonathan Poneman, President, Sub Pop Records

"The best messed-up love song you'll ever read."

—Dan Palladino and Amy Sherman-Palladino,
creators of *The Gilmore Girls*

Also by Joe Pernice

Meat Is Murder: A Novella

RIVERHEAD BOOKS

New York

It Feels So Good When I Stop

JOE PERNICE

RIVERHEAD BOOKS
Published by the Penguin Group
Penguin Group (USA) Inc.
375 Hudson Street, New York, New York 10014, USA
Penguin Group (Canada), 90 Eglinton Avenue East, Suite 700, Toronto, Ontario M4P 2Y3, Canada
(a division of Pearson Penguin Canada Inc.)
Penguin Books Ltd., 80 Strand, London WC2R 0RL, England
Penguin Group Ireland, 25 St. Stephen's Green, Dublin 2, Ireland (a division of Penguin Books Ltd.)
Penguin Group (Australia), 250 Camberwell Road, Camberwell, Victoria 3124, Australia
(a division of Pearson Australia Group Pty. Ltd.)
Penguin Books India Pvt. Ltd., 11 Community Centre, Panchsheel Park, New Delhi—110 017, India
Penguin Group (NZ), 67 Apollo Drive, Rosedale, North Shore 0632, New Zealand
(a division of Pearson New Zealand Ltd.)
Penguin Books (South Africa) (Pty.) Ltd., 24 Sturdee Avenue, Rosebank, Johannesburg 2196,
South Africa

Penguin Books Ltd., Registered Offices: 80 Strand, London WC2R 0RL, England

This is a work of fiction. Names, characters, places, and incidents either are the product of the author's imagination or are used fictitiously, and any resemblance to actual persons, living or dead, business establishments, events, or locales is entirely coincidental. The publisher does not have any control over and does not assume any responsibility for author or third-party websites or their content.

First Riverhead hardcover edition: August 2009
First Riverhead trade paperback edition: August 2010
Riverhead trade paperback ISBN: 978-1-59448-469-8

The Library of Congress has catalogued the Riverhead hardcover edition as follows:

Pernice, Joseph T., date.
    It feels so good when I stop : a novel / Joe Pernice.
        p.   cm.
    ISBN 978-1-59448-874-0
    I. Title.
PS3616.E74917   2009   2009013218
813'.6—dc22

PRINTED IN THE UNITED STATES OF AMERICA

10   9   8   7   6   5   4   3   2   1

For Laura and Sammy

This is the place where I made my best mistakes.

—*Elvis Costello*

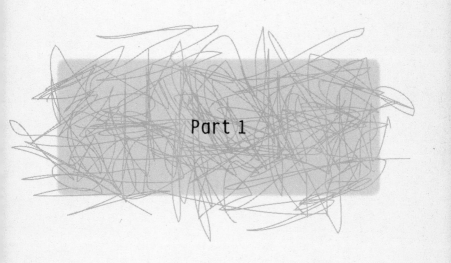

Part 1

October 1996

"I HAVE CANCER from working with boat glue. Lung cancer," James said, as if telling me he liked toast. Wheat toast. Just like that, thoughts of my troubles with Jocelyn receded.

"Jesus Christ, James, are you shitting me?" I asked, flicking my smoke to the sandy pavement, inches from the outer reaches of his yellow lawn. I thought, That's it. I'm quitting.

"I wish I was, my friend. I wish I was." He soothed his temples with the tips of his fingers.

"That's horrible. Does my sister know?"

"I haven't figured out how I'm going to tell her."

"Fuck me."

"Yeah, it's pretty bad. I should have taken better care of myself when I was young."

"But you're only thirty-eight, for chrissake."

I was thirteen years younger than James, but he could have easily pounded the living shit out of me. He was six feet two and looked like an off-brand version of the guy on the Brawny paper towel package. When he was on the upside of a sneeze, his lungs swelled like those of a whale preparing to dive. He fixed boats for a living. His arms were strung with an overkill of lean muscle. It was embarrassing.

"Yeah, well, anyway, I should have taken better care of myself. Take my advice"—he motioned with his chin toward the smoldering butt. A Century 21 For Sale sign squeaked in the breeze—"I always thought I'd have more time, you know? Now they tell me I'll be lucky to make forty." He leaned, defeated, against the equally terminal baby-blue Chevy Suburban with boat in tow. Both vehicles were still registered in my sister's name.

"What are you telling me here? I mean, are you like . . . ?" I couldn't bring myself to say it. He touched my shoulder, and it moved me that he, in his condition, was trying to comfort me.

"Am I what, dying?"

I nodded.

He inhaled deeply for strength. "Nah, I'm just fucking with you." He picked up my smoke and resuscitated it. "Come on. Give me a hand covering this prick."

I didn't need the mind-fuck, but I did need a place to stay; somewhere I wouldn't have to answer a lot of questions while I got my shit in a pile. If I had to be around someone, James was better than most. He'd rather fake cancer for a laugh than pick your brain.

"Get on the starboard side," he barked.

"Which side is that?"

"The one opposite me." A good chunk of his bust stuck out above the trailer-mounted boat. He unfolded a plastic tarp. "Hey, you hear the one about the faggot ensign that got busted down to seaman?"

"Yes."

"He got caught swabbing a rear admiral's poop deck. Get it?"

I nodded. With my smoke still burning in the crotch of his fingers, my sister's soon-to-be ex-husband pointed at me and said, "Seriously, the best advice I can give you is this: Die at the curb."

"Isn't that a Wesley Snipes movie?"

"If it isn't, it should be." He draped the tarp over the Switchcraft, showing as much respect for it as a living soldier would for a dead comrade. A sharp gust blew in from Opal Cove and passed through my hair, making me feel bald. James held down the billowing blue plastic. "Trust me," he said. "If you're walking alone along Tremont Street at two in the morning, and a car pulls up, and some dirtbag tells you to get in or he's going to shoot, well, fuck that noise. Tell him to shoot. If he had a gun, he would have been wagging it in your face already."

"Hmm," I said, trying to prompt the least passionate response from him. I wanted for us to finish covering the boat and for him to be on his way. I held a wily corner while he laced a nylon cord through aluminum eyelets that had been dulled by oxidation.

James and my sister Pamela were splitting custody of their only kid, an eighteen-month-old named Roy. I had already seen Roy make the same determined face James was making just then as we winterized the boat he had deluded himself into thinking he could afford.

"And if by some friggin' miracle he does have a gun, you're better off dying at the curb." James stopped lacing and pointed an X-Acto knife at me. "Because you know that fucker has something worse in mind for you." He looked into the middle distance and thought on it. "Some sick Viet Cong shit like breaking a glass rod in your cock or stuffing a yard of barbed wire up your ass." He made an upwardly thrusting motion with his hairy, balled-up hand. The place where his wedding band had been for six years was still lighter than the rest of him. I had hardly been in direct sunlight in the three days since Jocelyn and I got married.

"You want to be found like that, naked, stuffed in a fifty-gallon chemical drum in a storage shed in Revere? How do you think that would go over with Carl and Lucy?"

"Not so good."

"Not so good? They'd be friggin' crushed. Your mother would slit her own throat to kill the pain. And Carl? Well, shit, he'd let her."

Since those were my parents he was talking about, I started to gather up a comeback, but I just didn't have the energy to get into it with him.

James and I were never exactly friends. He was generally a decent guy. He'd jump in the icy river without thinking and save the drowning truck driver. But, fuck me, if you didn't agree with him when it came to what was what, he'd go on one of his correction trips and figuratively step on your throat until you declared yourself saved.

I guess I can understand on one level why Pamela was attracted to James. Older guy. Independent. Something to say—right or wrong—about everything. Physically imposing. Good father specimen. All Pamela wanted to be was a mother. She said so a number of times; said so with surety and—what seemed to me to be—a lack of ebullience. It was as if she'd said, "You know what? I want to take a cruise." I'm not sure why, but it was embarrassing for me to hear her talk about wanting to be a mother. I told her there were plenty of better things she could do with her life than be just a mother.

Pamela had barely enough gas in the tank to get through two years at Massasoitt Community College. Since the time she was twenty, she worked as an administrative assistant for the Town of Mashpee. Before she got mixed up with James, she dated electricians or guys who drove snowplows for the town. She was four years older than me, and for most of my life she looked out for me. When I got accepted to a "real" college, I started trying to treat her like I was the older one.

I faked a loud shiver, hoping it would jar James onto a topic with less spice. It was late October on Cape Cod, and I was underdressed. A shiver was easy to come by.

As he executed the moves of a complex, nautically themed knot, James said, "That's my real advice to you. Die. At. Thee. Curb."

I started longingly squeezing one of the boat's white vinyl headrests. As it slowly sprang back to its full size, I replayed one of the many dry-run breakups between Jocelyn and me.

I had gone down to New York to visit her for the weekend. Sunday was Father's Day. The holiday was like a giant elephant turd in the room. Even dead, her old man was remarkably good at being a tyrant. She never got the chance to tell him off the way she had no problem telling me off.

We finally scraped ourselves from bed late on Saturday afternoon. We took the F train from Brooklyn uptown to Second Avenue and had lunch at B&H Dairy. A giant fan drove a vortex of warm air into the room, overwhelming the tiny space. Our napkins kept flying off the counter. The meal started out tenderly enough. We were debating which salad was better, whitefish or tuna. Before Jocelyn was able to convince me that tuna was where it's at, she ditched the argument altogether. She said she was just as big a hypocritical asshole as me for eating what was once another living thing. I brought up corn, and wasn't that a living thing? She said she didn't feel great about killing anything—plant or animal—for food. I told her to give me a fucking break. Things got meaner and more personal very quickly.

Just because all sorts of shit happens all the time in New York doesn't mean people don't like seeing it when it does. A couple fighting in a restaurant is almost as entertaining as a medical emergency or a fire.

I kept telling Jocelyn to keep her voice down. She told me to grow up. She said people in "adult" relationships yell, and sometimes the yelling takes place in public. I told her to lighten up for once. She slammed some money on the counter and told me to go fuck myself. I told her I'd do just that. She was wearing a white German Air Force tank top and a denim miniskirt with no stockings. As she got up to leave, I could hear the back of her thighs peel off the revolving vinyl seat like a Colorform separating from its glossed cardboard tableau. I finished my bowl of mushroom barley soup, trolling for comradeship in the droopy faces of two old guys speaking Polish.

I mumbled all the way to Port Authority and caught the next bus back to Amherst. I renewed my often-broken vow to remain broken up. When I got home there were eight messages on my machine from Jocelyn. They ran the gamut, from viciously accusatory to weepy and contrite. She even went as far as confessing to having "hooked up" with a coworker named Geoff; he pronounced it "Joff." She said it was after the Freedy Johnston gig at Fez. Geoff told her he knew she was spoken for, but he could let himself fall in love with her, no problem. Just say the word. I knew she was probably lying, but I couldn't help imagining the worst. In her final good-bye, she begged me to make the shrinking remainder of my life remarkable because I deserved no less. She asked me not to call her because I had to let her get beyond me.

The fuck I did.

I caught the next bus back to Port Authority and showed up exhausted and crazy at her apartment in Park Slope. She was a beautiful mess. She'd just dyed her hair the bloodiest red she'd worn to date. She looked like a *Breathless*-era Jean Seberg with a mortal head wound. She asked me what I was doing there. I said I wanted to tell her in person that I knew it wouldn't make her happy, but if it did, she and Geoff could fuck each other deep into their twilight years. She slapped my face. My glasses came to rest beneath a small red stepladder used for holding potted plants. She broke down. She threw herself into my arms and begged me not to cut her loose. She

Joe Pernice

said she could be good. Just give her a chance. I told her she was good. I am? You're the greatest. No, you are. I rubbed the back of her neck, twisting the fine underhairs into forgetful knots. Within two minutes, we were fantastically make-up-fucking each other back into our ever-deepening mess.

I COULD SEE by the discomfort on James's face that he could see the discomfort on my own face.

"I sure as fuck don't want to live here anymore," he said. "But you're welcome to crash until the place sells."

I started to feel guilty for thinking he was anything but bighearted.

Seagulls passing overhead blitzed the partially covered boat. James reached up to strangle any one of them floating high above the spindly treetops. "Friggin' sky rats." He wiped the bird shit with the sleeve of his Dress Gordon flannel shirt. "So, Pamela tells me you and Jocelyn got hitched Friday, and you're already splitting up?"

"Pretty messed up, huh?"

He pulled firmly on the nylon cord to test the integrity of his knot. "I don't know. Marriage and divorce are two of the best things a man can do for himself."

IT WAS DARK by seven o'clock. Two months earlier East Falmouth had been a madhouse of vacationers who couldn't afford to buy or rent farther out on the island. Now the town was nearly deserted.

Before heading back to his furnished separation pad in Orleans, James slipped out and bought me a case of Miller High Lifes, a pack of Marlboro reds, and an orange lighter.

"You can't smoke 'em if you can't friggin' light 'em, right?"

"Thanks, man, but I don't think I have enough cash to cover all this."

"Eh, don't sweat it. It's not like I gave you one of my livers." He swung the case of beer to me like we were members of the bucket brigade. "Welcome aboard."

I SAT ON the screen porch in the crisp autumn night and watched a few random lights reflected on Opal Cove just beyond a row of ranch houses and summer cottages opposite my sister's.

When I'd bolted from our honeymoon suite at the Gramercy Park Hotel, I left a note on the floor where Jocelyn would see it. It said, "I'm sorry."

I drained a beer and swallowed back a belch. From outer space they can shoot a pimple on a nomad's bag while he's taking a leak in the desert. Hiding out on Cape Cod did not exactly qualify me for "off the grid" status. If Jocelyn wanted to find me, she could.

I lit the next smoke with the end of the last one, then extinguished the butt in the backwash at the bottom of a bottle. I could hear a single boat motor shrinking in volume as its propeller chewed the water's epidermis, pushing both boat and contents in the direction of Gay Head.

I drank another beer, and was about to go inside for the night, when I caught sight of a shadowy form moving up the street. It appeared to be hugging its midsection as if it were privately suffering from indigestion or a knife wound. I wasn't overwhelmingly compelled to involve myself in anyone else's trauma, but if whoever-the-fuck-it-was died while I was hiding inside, well, shit, what kind of person would that make me? I'd stay put until it passed out of my airspace. After that, it was someone else's problem.

When the body entered the circle of streetlight adjacent to my sister's driveway, I could tell it was a woman. Her Kelly green track jacket and purple Doc Martens hummed. She stopped momentarily and straightened up when she spotted me watching her from the porch. She slipped back into the darkness, and when she emerged, she was coming up the walkway, straight for me. I was more surprised than anything. I mean, if something happened—unless she had a gun or something—I felt pretty confident that I could take her. I tightened my grip on an empty bottle just in case.

She came up to the bottom step. I made her to be in her mid-thirties. She had a round face, capped by a grown-out black China-doll bob. Her steamy breath left her in truncated puffs. Both legs of her jeans were wet up to just below the knee, as if she'd been standing on the beach long after the tide had begun to roll in.

Her voice was raspy, like Brenda Vaccaro's. "Who are you?" she asked.

I could tell she wasn't straddling the peak of Mount Shitfaced, but she was either on her way up or at the corresponding point coming down the other side. I was actually slightly amused. "Who am I?"

"Mmm."

"Who are you?"

She nodded, like that was a reasonable answer. "Marie." She pointed in the direction she'd been moving. "From there."

I looked at the blemished blackness into which she was headed. "That's nice."

"It was." She pointed at me. "You got another one of those?"

"Of what, beer? Smoke?"

"Both."

"Sure," I said begrudgingly. As a drinker and a smoker, I knew the code: If your supply is visible—which sadly mine was—you always share when asked. I loosened my grip on the empty bottle and handed her a full one. I didn't think she was going to pound it on the spot. I watched the beer pass from one receptacle to another, restricted only by gravity and the unfortunate narrowness of the bottle's opening.

She swapped the cold, empty bottle for a cigarette.

"You need a light?"

"Mmm." She cupped the flame and leaned into it. The backs of her hands were a multicolored filigree of tattoo ink. "Thanks."

"No problem."

And then she split.

My eyes followed the glowing orange tip down the street until it was too small to see. Welcome to Cape Cod, I thought.

I ARRANGED MY makeshift bed on the barren living room floor, which was covered with a sandy, mange-afflicted gold shag rug. I chose a spot close to a small color television perched on a milk crate that James had set up in the early days of his own separation. I covered myself with a moving blanket and hunkered down.

I couldn't sleep, so I started jerking a disinterested dick towards a distant conclusion. I flipped through the wank bank, finally stopping at a love scene starring me and a Bay State Games bronze-medalist pole-vaulter who was in the same Major British Writers study group as me. I couldn't remember if her name was Catherine or Kathleen, but she went by Cat or Kat, so it didn't matter. Jocelyn kept crashing the vignette no matter how hard I tried to write her out of it. And then I stopped trying.

Jocelyn was sitting across from me in an empty bar in Hadley. A torrential downpour was in full swing.

It was close to midnight. Our relationship was new. We weren't even on farting terms yet. We planned on walking through the muddy cornfields beyond the back parking lot, but we never made it. "I'm Your Puppet" was playing on the jukebox. Jocelyn was singing along out of tune. She filled her cheeks with Wild Turkey and motioned for my mouth to meet hers in the middle. When she kissed me, she let some of the booze drain into me.

As I was coming, it felt almost as good as the real thing. But it had a lonely finish, like a nonalcoholic beer.

IN THE WINTER OF 1994, I graduated from UMass after four and a half years with a BA in English. I did pretty average; a lot worse than I might have done if I had given the tiniest of fucks about school. I decided to dick around until the summer and not think about my limited prospects, my withering University Health Insurance, and the looming crush of student loan repayment. I picked up three shifts waiting tables at a mediocre Italian restaurant in Amherst called Esposito's. I ended up working there for almost two years.

Richie could be charming as all hell, whether he was sober or not. Being decent-looking didn't hurt. He was decidedly closer to a Dennis than a Randy Quaid. He'd been a waiter at Esposito's for a couple of years when

I got there. I shadowed him my first week. I liked him right off the bat. We both played guitar and were into a lot of the same music. Neither of us gave a fuck if it was Doris Day or the Frogs. If it was good music, it was good music. On my first night we made tentative plans to do some four-track recording together. He said he had written a ton of songs and already had the best band name: the Young Accuser. He said he'd gotten it from a newspaper article he read about Michael Jackson. All he needed was a band.

"No shit," Richie said as he showed me how to fold a napkin into a swan. "I've read more books than any professor I ever had." I never would have made a statement remotely as bold. I knew my education was held together by large fugues and obvious holes. "I'd go toe-to-toe with any of them and win." Such braggadocio made Richie rub as many people (men) the wrong way as it did (women) the right. I sensed almost immediately that his whole "I couldn't conform to the bullshit academic mold" claptrap was mostly a smoke screen because he couldn't hack it. It was one of his flaws that made him approachable to me.

The owner-chef at Esposito's was a prick named Lello, whose entire personality can be extrapolated from the following: (1) he loved cocaine even more than he appeared to love himself; (2) literally minutes into my first shift, a black waitress named Suzanne called him on his racist, sexist shit and stormed out. The restaurant was going to be packed because it was Valentine's Day weekend. Lello was so furious he nearly blew a testicle. He ordered the entire staff into the kitchen, grabbed the biggest, blackest iron skillet off the rack, and screamed, "From now on, whoever calls this pan something other than Suzanne can get right the fuck out."

I felt like a real shit for not having the backbone to tell him to fuck himself on the spot. I dusted off the "I really need the money" excuse and fell for it. In the end, when I finally did quit Esposito's, I merely stopped showing up. In the men's room there's a urinal named Kenneth. The one next to that is named after me.

At the end of the night, after Richie and I performed our setup duties for the next day, we sat at the enormous black marble bar, each drinking an allotted half-priced domestic draft beer. I was still blowing smoke here and there about how much I'd like to tell this Lello character to jam his job up his fat ass.

Richie made it easy for me to stay weak and still come off like I had principles. "You can't quit. If you do, the wop wins." He ordered two neat shots of Jack Daniel's from the bartender, Rita. Her arms were as hairy as any man's.

I pretended to be watching the pour. "Wow," I said, "those are really something."

"Rita knows how to fix a healthy drink." He slid a ten across the bar.

Rita winked. "If these won't get the taste of come out

of your mouth, I don't know what will." She slid Richie two fives change. He stuffed one of the fives into her tip snifter. We toasted my survival of the first night, then slammed our Jacks. I could feel my esophagus beginning to molt.

"Yeah," Richie said, "you can't quit after one night. Give it a week."

With quiet contempt, I searched the dining room for Lello. He was showing a veteran waiter the "real" right way to do something.

Rita wiped the bar in front of us with her Cain and Abel arms, then disappeared back into the kitchen.

"Man," I whispered, "what's up with her arms?"

"Arms, nothing." Richie leaned over the bar to make sure Rita wasn't kneeling down just out of sight. "I swear to God, her bush is so big and dense. It's like she's wearing gorilla panties."

I cracked up.

"It's like an enormous crown of black broccoli. No, shit, some topiary guy should shape that thing into some low-income fucking housing." Richie rattled off another few hilarious suggestions for what should be done with Rita's pubic hair. He was killing me.

Rita's head appeared through a window in the swinging kitchen doors.

"Chill," Richie said. "She'd be bummed if she heard us."

"Really?"

Rita started restocking the beer fridge. She poked her head over the bar. She could sense something was up. "What the fuck did you do?"

Richie smiled like a guilty schoolboy whose tracks were pretty well covered. "What are you talking about?"

"Exactly," she accused. "With that grin on your face? You must have done something."

"You're paranoid is what you are."

"You'd better steer clear of this one," she said to me.

"Just do your job," Richie barked.

Rita flipped him off, then refilled our drinks when the coast was clear.

A few of the frazzled waitstaff were reorganizing the dining room at high speed. Patti Smith's "Frederick" was coming over the sound system. A chubby, middle-aged waiter named Dennis was fitting a matchbook under the leg of a table with polio.

Richie called over to him. "Hey, Menace. You know the band Anal Cunt?"

"Sounds yummy," Dennis said, camping it up for us. He had nico-tinted, thinning blond hair and acne scars on his temples.

Richie and Dennis were friends. They were big basketball fans and used to go watch UMass games together before the team got good and tickets scarce. I hated basketball. Too much contact with other people's sweat.

"They have a tune called 'Pepe, the Gay Waiter.' I think you might like it."

"Tape it for me." Dennis meant it. Richie meant it when he said he would. Dennis pushed on the table to gauge whether it had been cured.

"You think Camby's gonna go pro?" Richie asked.

"I would. Why risk millions for a degree from UMass? What if Dr. J had stayed and blown a knee or something?"

"Bet you've blown a few knees in your day, huh, Menace?"

Dennis chortled, then moved to the next table, also checking it for wobbliness. It was after midnight, just about that time when restaurant people want to get the fuck home, get the fuck drunk, get the fuck fucked, or any combination of the three. Richie took a stolen langostino from his breast pocket and popped into his mouth.

"Yeah, you can't quit yet," he said. "Stick around. Make a little scratch and rob that fat fuck blind." He spit out a speck of shellfish, which I could still feel minutes after I'd wiped it from my cheek. "You know anyone who needs to rent a room?"

A MONTH LATER Richie and I were sharing the second-floor apartment in a melting Victorian on Amity Street. A few more years of student tenants, and the whole house would need to be gutted or demolished.

When I moved in, my room smelled like a Habitrail cage. The windowsills were coated with a gritty plaque that made my nails black. The light fixture on the ceiling was full of roasted bugs. There was a poster of three shapely women in bathing suits—their six breasts abreast to form the Budweiser symbol—tacked up, alarmingly, at a height corresponding to that of an average man's crotch. I removed the poster—carefully—revealing a series of steel-toed-boot holes. When I asked Richie if he knew what it was all about, he said the previous tenant, Gary, was trying to hide the booze-inspired damage so that he wouldn't lose his security deposit. Richie suggested I put the poster back up when it was time for me to move out.

Gary also left behind a twin mattress because it had been there when he moved in. Perfectly acceptable shit-pit protocol: New Guy inherits Old Guy's cast-offs, milks them for use, and leaves them behind for Next Guy. I removed the gray fitted sheet. The mattress fabric was stained so extensively, it looked like a batik tapestry hippie girls hang on their dorm walls. I flipped it over, and it wasn't as bad. That was the side I slept on.

The bathroom was a dewy terrarium of unplanned growth, and Richie's room looked like the inside of a fourth-hand customized van he wasn't planning on selling anytime soon.

We hung out mostly in the kitchen because it was more spacious than the other rooms combined. It was connected to the rest of the apartment by a dark, lumpy hallway the length of a landing strip at an international airport. My rent was two-fifty plus utilities. I couldn't see myself being able to afford it for too long.

The property manager was a guy named Arn who had lived in Amherst most of his fifty-odd years. Arn was marginally sexier than Ernest Borgnine. His family had come over from the Ukraine when he was a kid, but he still spoke with a heavy accent. He lived alone in the casket-sized apartment someone with a flare for architectural discontinuity had added to the first floor.

"Let's see if Geppetto wants a hit," Richie said. We were standing on the failing back porch, getting clobbered by purple-haired bong hits. Richie yelled down to the garage where Arn was working on fuck-knows-what. (He definitely wasn't milling new crown molding.) A circular saw went mute. Arn's bloodshot nose—followed by the rest of his bloodshot face—appeared in the garage doorway. Richie hoisted an imaginary broomstick-thick joint to his mouth and took a greedy toke. He knew how to make it look delicious because he meant it. The Arn-man almost always cameth.

We got high as pipers. The kind of stoned where you think you might puke. It was a good thing I was standing, because an all-weather patio chair that had looked so inviting minutes before was starting to resemble a wolf trap.

" 'You' is a real ball-breaking bitch," Richie said.

"Wha?" I asked. I hadn't noticed the music at all until

Richie pointed to the floor. After that it came at me like lasers in stereo. From the apartment below ours, Bono Vox bellowed that he couldn't live with you or without you. It was a tough spot to be in. And though Bono tried to sound like a man in control of the situation, it was obvious that "You" held all the cards.

" 'You' should make up her goddamn mind."

"What if 'You' is a dude?" I asked. "All rock stars like a cock every now and then."

"Then 'You' should make up his goddamn mind."

"It's definitely a broad," Arn said, death-row serious. Those were the first words he'd offered up voluntarily, maybe ever. Richie and I weed-laughed. Arn failed to see the humor in any of it. He tried to scratch an itch deep in the geometric center of his head. Richie started imitating him. My chest burned from laughing and coughing. Arn finally left us there when it was clear we weren't about to stop laughing. He descended the stairs like a deep-fried Slinky toy. Richie kept imitating him after he was gone, rubbing the roof of his mouth maniacally while making increasingly more retarded-looking faces. I begged him to quit it, but he wouldn't.

I WOKE UP on my stomach, using my foot to either feel the rug next to me for Jocelyn or defend myself from her.

I must have been moving frantically in my sleep because I burned the knuckles on a couple of my toes. I was trying to decide whether or not I should sit up and investigate them when I heard a very un-Brooklyn, all-natural cracking noise. I rolled onto my side. A large maple tree filled most of the picture window, naked in the wind like the Statue of Liberty stripped of her green clothes and skin.

Fuck New York.

I wondered if it was possible to avoid it for the rest of my life. A guy can say with some degree of certainty while passing through What's-his-nuts, Montana, on a bus, that, God willing, he'll never be back that way. But for him to make that claim about New York City—even if he doesn't have a wife there—is hubristic.

I picked at the wound where the carpet had separated from the baseboard. For the time being at least, I wasn't going anywhere near New York. I had done my part by prying open the lioness's mouth. There was no way I was going to stick my fucking head in. I rolled onto my back and gave in to my growing hunger for a cigarette.

The TV was still cooking from the night before. I jacked the volume from zero to full with an unbridled, upward flick of the toe. A long, distorted trumpet blast from an elephant spanked the bare walls of the empty living room.

"Nooooo," I pleaded with the TV. I turned the volume down before the set could explode. My eye was caught by a visually pleasing, grainy 1960s nature documentary. The auteur was clearly a fan of the Marx Brothers' *Duck Soup*. Some elephants were dancing and laughing as they sprayed muddy water over one another's wrinkled hulls. An orchestra of piccolos, trombones, xylophones, and tympani swelled to a crescendo as a calf wading shoulder-deep in the slop vanished beneath celebratory salvos. I was transfixed, like a toddler at his first puppet show.

In the next scene an alpha male gibbon was about to join his face to the private parts of the monkey of his choice. This was no ordinary prelude to a kiss. The alpha strode in super slow-mo toward his mark. She stood on her haunches, her business end swollen and red like an Italian cherry pepper. The alpha puckered up, advancing with a brutal authority not witnessed on film since Bogie first kissed Bacall. Just before the moment of impact, the editor cut to a shot of a chimpanzee called Henry the Eighth tenderizing a piece of fruit by firing it down at a rock from high up in a tree.

"C'mon, Henry. C'mon, old boy," the overdubbed narrator cheered.

An overdubbed chimp's voice squealed in response. The chemistry between man and beast was so convincing, I could imagine them perched on the same limb or BBC soundstage.

"I am not an animal," I said. I had another smoke, then dozed back to sleep.

When I woke for the second time, my breath smelled

like a bum's pants. I got up and headed for the can. I felt hungover, but I was just decompressing from the bender of having deserted my wife.

At least Pamela and James don't seem to hate each other anymore, I thought. By mistake, I opened the closet next to the bathroom. It was empty except for some universally bluish gray floor lint and a coat hanger with a paper-covered fuselage.

Everything in the bathroom—the toilet, tub, tiles and sink—was a faded pink and well past its prime. Five grand in improvements might have made them fifteen on resale. Pamela said getting rid of the place and moving on with her life as soon as possible were her top priorities. She and Roy moved into a newish two-bedroom condo in Plymouth. She wanted to be closer to our parents, which seemed like a terrible idea to me.

I owned no property to speak of. I had reluctantly moved from Amherst, Massachusetts, to Brooklyn to live with Jocelyn two weeks before we eloped. All I brought with me was a Gibson Hummingbird acoustic guitar and a soft maroon suitcase. The only remotely durable good Jocelyn and I owned together was a Mini Shop-Vac we'd bought from the Astor Place Kmart. I waited until we got to the front of the line before I gave her my half of the cash. Jocelyn took the money, and it felt like my arm went with it. She handed the checkout girl her Visa, and it came back bloody: our domestic hymen officially torn to shreds.

The pink paint on the bathroom walls was many shades brighter where a mirrored medicine cabinet had hung. It was a relief not to have to look at myself. I started to feel like a genuine gaping asshole, picturing Jocelyn levitating along Twenty-third Street back to our honeymoon suite, gripping a six-pack and some takeout: She swings the heavy, fireproof door open. I don't tango naked out of the bathroom with a fresh rubber in my teeth. I don't glide back from the ice machine with a bottle of champagne rising from the bucket like an emerald swan. Just as my getaway train lurches away from the platform, Jocelyn reads my note and falls off the bone like piping-hot Peking duck.

I gathered some foul-tasting saliva to the front of my mouth, spat into the sink, and examined it for blood. During some of our breakups, I had seen Jocelyn do things like bite herself on the back of the hand while crying, pull out keepsake-sized tethers of hair, and defenestrate objects of varying worth from her fifth-floor apartment. I feared this time I might have killed her.

It's not your fucking fault. If she kills herself over this, she's got bigger fucking problems than your leaving her. My conviction was wobbly, like I was the sounding board for a happened-upon old acquaintance who knew I knew he knew he'd always been half a prick in my book. But the dubious logic of my self-directed pep talk seemed to possess the power of temporary exoneration. And although

I had neither studied nor pretended to have studied any Zen philosophy, I decided in that bathroom to begin living in the moment.

I looked deeply "into" the place where the medicine cabinet had been and chanted, "Medi-cine cabi-net. Medi-cine cabi-net."

I opened both taps and let the water run from tan to clear, per James's instructions. I started to wonder how much your average medicine cabinet goes for. Thirty bucks? Forty? Thirty bucks seemed reasonable for a medicine cabinet. I traced its absence many times. I passed my hand through its void. "Medi-cine cabi-net." I started to wonder who got custody of the medicine cabinet that had once been there. And did they fight over it? The possibility of Pamela and James going to war over a thirty-dollar medicine cabinet made me feel like I had regained consciousness on the concourse of a dead midwestern shopping mall.

Fuck the fucking Buddhists.

I peeked under the sink for a razor left behind in the move. A shave might change my world completely. I ran the shower, giving the water time to get clean and hot. I weighed the chances of Jocelyn and me someday being friends. It was un-fucking-likely. She and I were strictly scorched earthlings. If we didn't get back together this time, I was sure I'd never see her again. I stepped into the shower and brushed my teeth with my finger.

"Motherfuck." I clawed what was left of the soap from the soap-dish. It was like a dry sliver of Romano cheese. A small window in the shower wall promised to open on the backyard. When I tried to unlock it, the fixture broke free from the water-rotten sash and bounced around the tub.

"Are you kidding me?"

I tapped into the reserve strength in my legs to raise the paint-sealed window. I stuck my head out the window into the brisk sunlight, half expecting the guillotine's blade to finish me off.

On the far side of the clothes-dryer vent, against the toolshed, leaned the forlorn Huffy Sweet Thunder bicycle Pamela had gotten for her tenth birthday. I sized it up, encouraged by the legend of the great George Jones piloting a ride-on lawn mower miles into town to score booze. George Jones is a genius, and I am not. It was only fitting that I should have to pedal a child's dilapidated toy.

I got out of the shower and began drying myself with my dirty underwear, the only piece of clothing I could spare. When the pitiful trunks could drink no more, I swung them over the curtain rod. If I was going to be there for any length of time, me and Sweet Thunder were going to have to make a run into town for supplies.

AS I STEPPED OUT into the backyard, I could feel the pores in my face tighten. I took the half bag of cashews from a pocket of my denim jacket. When these nuts were growing on the tree in Iran or Turkey or wherever the fuck it was, did they ever imagine this is how they'd end up? I lifted the bag to my mouth and chugged. The dormant back lawn was as tough as an equestrian brush. The sound of it abrading the soles of my shoes was plangent accompaniment to the crunching in my head.

I grabbed Sweet Thunder by a handle grip, leaned it toward the ground, and surveyed the damage. Every visible inch of chrome and the pink-and-white color scheme was freckled with rust. The quilted pink vinyl seat was split at the rear, and when I banged it with my hand to see if it was sound, it coughed crumbs of brittle foam. The tires still held some air, but their painted whitewalls were gray and weakened by craquelure. I gave the bike a good hard shake. Nothing fell off, so I fell on.

My knees banged against my elbows as I pedaled away from the safety of the house's gravitational pull. The rusted chain moaned like a dolphin tortured to within an inch of its life. The whole machine—myself included—was so shaky, the rear wheel threatened to overtake the front.

I stopped at the junction where Opal Cove Road, my sister's residential street, intersected Plymouth Street, the town's main thoroughfare. During the summer, traffic on Plymouth Street slowed to a crawl. But in the off-season, laid-off house painters, handymen, and half-in-the-bag drywall hangers could do fifty-plus and almost never kill anyone. I turned up my collar and started left toward town.

There was a Great Atlantic Job Lot supply store a couple miles down the road. They sold everything from heavy-duty steel HVAC couplings coated with neoprene to boxes of counterfeit Cocoa Puffs cereal.

I was as aerodynamic as a pug-nosed city bus. I must have looked like a lunatic, my body absorbing the tiny bicycle as we moved forward with just enough momentum to remain upright. A cop driving in the opposite direction toasted my effort with a Dunkin' Donuts medium coffee.

"Fucking great."

I crested a mild incline. As I coasted down the long far side, I opened my mouth and let the nippy headwind inflate my lungs and do some of my breathing for me. My hands and face were freezing, but my torso was damp with sweat. It was like having to take a spectacular piss while dying of thirst.

To my right, the beach was peaceful and empty, except for the odd bundled-up elderly couple and driftwood-gnawing dog. The late-October sun was still bright enough to soften the color of the water that had already begun to sour toward a winter gray. On my left, marine equipment suppliers, bait-and-tackle shops, scuba outfitters, and rickety, lucrative clam shacks were shut down until Memorial Day. I battled the wind and followed the shoreline for the rest of the trip, past sand-blown beach parking lots with gates locked and signs that read Closed for Season. In the distance on the left, I could see Great Atlantic Job Lot's giant yellow sign. I bargained with my clamoring respiratory system: You get this bike to that sign, then we smoke.

WHEN I MET Jocelyn I knew within minutes I was going to either marry her or completely destroy my life trying. It never occurred to me that both things could happen.

On the morning that kicked off the era known as Mein Jocelyn Kampf, I woke to the smell of perfectly good coffee ruined with hazelnut. As I passed the bathroom, I could hear Richie in the shower, singing Mudhoney's "Touch Me I'm Sick." I had a good idea what constituted a successful night in his mind, and he must have had one because he was singing and retching, instead of just the latter.

"Hey, cunt-lip, make sure you rinse the tub," I said, a wishful thought at best even if he could have heard me. "I don't want your bum chum's crabby pubes sticking to my feet." Like most guy friends who live together, Richie and I could sling it pretty raw at home. We meant only about a quarter of it. If what we said in the privacy of our own home was overheard on the outside, we'd be tried as hate criminals.

I stopped short in the kitchen doorway. An attractive woman I'd never seen before was sitting at our rusty chrome-and-Formica table.

"Sorry about that. I didn't know anyone else was here."

"So gay bashing's okay only if the right people hear it?"

Here we go, I thought. If I had known her, I would have said, Yes, it's okay. If she had known me, she would have known I was just fucking around.

"We always talk that way to each other. It was just a joke."

"I'm kidding," she said. "I'm kidding." She slapped her knee. "Touchy, aren't we?"

I liked her instantly.

"Thanks. Just what I need bright and early."

She seemed proud of herself for messing with my head so successfully. She tried to untangle a fuck-knot in her hair. I made sure my T-shirt was covering the fly of my boxers as I passed her on my way to the sink. The dishwater in the grubby Rubbermaid tub was greasy and orange from a Bolognese sauce Lello had plagiarized from a larger talent. I fished out a spoon and a pink mug encircled by a bracelet of cartoon bunnies going down on each other. I tested the shower-weakened stream for warmth and squeezed onto the sponge enough Palmolive to wash a car. I peeked over my shoulder at her. An unlit smoke swung from her bottom lip.

"Can I bum one of those?"

She tapped the top of the pack against the instep of her hand. A low-pitched clang signaled the end of Richie's shower. She lit two cigarettes and fixed one in the ashtray so its filter pointed to the empty seat across from her. A bottle of Wild Turkey that had been half-empty the previous evening was now completely empty. I poured myself what was left of the coffee and took a seat.

"So you're the roommate," she said.

"So I'm the roommate."

She said her name was Josie—or at least that was the name she went by because she hated her real name.

"How bad can it be?"

"Pretty bad."

Richie screamed through the last line of the song three times until he got it just right. Then he started coughing violently.

"Yup, he's a real trip, all right," I said with an astonishment-veneered pride.

"Oh, I'm discovering that pretty quick."

A portable turntable hi-fi unit from the seventies sat on a filing cabinet next to the table. A record was still spinning from the night before. I yanked the cord from the wall socket and stopped the record with the fat of my fist.

"Do you know this record?" I picked up the jacket to Nick Drake's *Five Leaves Left*.

"I didn't until last night. This morning, technically." She touched her face nervously, aware she'd revealed too much.

"What did you think of it? Pretty great, no?"

"Oh, my God, yes. I can't believe I'd never heard of him."

"Nobody has. They never will because the music business is fucked." Everything I knew about how fucked up the music business was came from a story about Fugazi I'd skimmed in *Magnet*.

"Suicide, right?"

"Pills," I said.

"That's how I'd do it."

"Depends on the pills. Imagine trying to overdose on speed." I'd taken speed exactly zero times, but I was talking like speed and me were old adversaries.

"I wouldn't know. I don't do drugs."

Smooth move, Ex-Lax.

"Can I have a look at that?" she asked. I handed her the record jacket. There was a hickey close to her elbow. She touched each title as she read it. "'River Man.' That song is so spooky. We listened to it like fifty times in a row."

"I know, right? The way the strings start out so legato." I let the word *legato* hang out there to lure her into asking me if I was musician. She didn't bite.

"Totally spooky," she said. Then she did something horrible. She started to scat to her tone-deafened inter-

Joe Pernice

pretation of the melody to "River Man." It was chilling in its unqualified and grotesque sincerity. And it went on too long. She finally grabbed her hair in frustration, as if the song she couldn't get out of her head were "Dancing on the Ceiling" or anything by Mike and the Mechanics.

Richie breezed into the kitchen, still buttoning up his Esposito's embroidered white oxford. He growled like a he-man when he saw Josie. He pulled her to her feet by her belt buckle and kissed her hard before she could protest. Then she was all his.

"Mmmmmmmm," they moaned in unison, like they were eating from the neck of the same caribou. While they kissed, Richie's hands moved up the back of her bare thighs and disappeared in the leg openings of her cut-off shorts. He grabbed two handfuls of ass and lifted her off her feet. She locked her legs around him. The whole scene was fucking gross. I tilted my chair back like a bored chain-smoking sixth-grader.

"Should I leave?"

They peeled apart like the halves of a developing Polaroid photo about to reveal the image of two infatuated people fucking.

"I'm the one who has to leave," Richie said, all lovey-dovey, still staring into Josie's eyes. I thought he was going to call her Poopsie or Snuggle Buns. "The wop's got a hair across his ass for me because two of my tables sent their braciole back last night."

"Stupid braciole," Josie said like a disappointed kindergartner.

Richie snorted and stared menacingly at her. "But I'll see *you* later," he said, and went for her belt again. She tried to elude him with some over-the-top dance steps. She was an all-too-willing participant in the embarrassing theater of it.

"Unhand me, you brute. I'll cry rape." She swatted the air with *Five Leaves Left*. "Back! Back!" she said like a lion trainer.

Richie got serious. "Whoa, whoa, whoa! That's an original Hannibal Records release you're holding there."

Josie came down. "Sorry." She surrendered the jacket.

Richie looked it over, at first for damage, then simply to admire it and the larger idea of Nick Drake. "Man, to play like that, the guy must have made a deal with the devil."

"It's like he was superhuman or something," Josie said.

Richie was stunned, like he'd just answered his doorbell to find Ed McMahon standing there with a giant cardboard check. "You know this record?"

"What, are you kidding?" Josie asked.

"No. Nobody knows Nick Drake." He turned to me. "Is this fucking cool or what? I finally meet a hot girl who has halfway decent taste in music."

Josie got up and ran to the bathroom. She slammed the door, and the towel rack fell to the floor.

Richie was confused. "What the fuck?"

"Dude," I whispered, "she said you guys were listening to Nick Drake all night."

Richie's face showed a different kind of concern. Either very small missing pieces of the night before were coming back to him or very large ones were not.

"Did you fuck her?" He didn't answer. He made the slow, strategizing walk to the bathroom door. I took a cigarette from Josie's pack and lit it.

"Is everything okay in there?" Richie asked. No answer. "Josie?"

"I'm fine," she said.

"You don't sound fine."

"Well, I am." She flushed the toilet.

Richie waited until it died down. "Are you sure?"

"Yes." The faucet went on, then off. "You should just go to work."

"I don't want to leave you like this."

"Go. I'm okay."

"You sure?" No answer. "You're sure you're okay?"

"Yes."

"Well, only if you're sure."

"I am."

"But you'll come by the restaurant so I can see you before you head back?" Josie didn't answer.

It sucked for me to witness the whole thing. Richie really was a good guy, but every so often an innocent got chewed up in his gears.

"Okay? You'll swing by the restaurant before you go?"

"Sure," Josie said.

Richie had probably been banking on some quick, pre-dinner-rush skull in the alley behind Esposito's. Now, if Josie showed up at all, he'd have to hide in the walk-in freezer until she left.

"Okay," he said. "I'll see you later. I hope you feel better." He walked back to the kitchen at a noticeably fast clip. He swept his keys up off the table.

"What about her?" I whispered.

"Just wait here until her ride shows up, please?"

"Christ." Richie dashed out the back door. I could feel the kitchen quieting down, like a placid body of water that had just finished swallowing a cruise ship. I polished off most of the smoke before Josie emerged from the bathroom. Here eyes were puffy, and her nose was pink. She took the seat across from me and started sobbing. I touched her shoulder on the place where her bra strap was digging into her skin.

Her girlfriend knocked on the screen door.

"It's open," I said.

Josie ran to her girlfriend and gave her a weepy hug. My future wife scowled at me from over Josie's shoulder. "What the fuck did you do to her?" Jocelyn demanded, holding Josie up so she wouldn't leak through the floor.

I LET SWEET THUNDER recover against a chain-link cage filled with empty propane tanks, and went inside the

Great Atlantic Job Lot. A true connoisseur of food can take a bite of the house specialty and identify its ingredients. I took one whiff and detected PVC vinyl, rubber cement, mothballs, a hint of tarragon, mesquite wood charcoal, and Absorbine Junior muscle rub.

A wind-battered elderly woman wearing an airbrush-on-white Robert Goulet concert sweatshirt stood at the only activated register. A tablecloth-sized piece of heavy clear plastic hung by its four corners from the high ceiling and served as a catch basin for whatever was dripping down into it. A length of rubber surgical tubing punctured the amniotic bulge and shunted the liquid out of sight through the "Employees Only" door. I grabbed a shopping cart and got down to business.

"Hello," I said to Goulet.

"Uh-huh."

I negotiated the narrow aisles, finding in logical order a twelve-pack of white tube socks; a six-pack of no-name briefs; a seven-pack of no-name T-shirts; a camouflaged knit hunter's hat and gloves; a gray polyester hooded sweatshirt; a tube of green Close-Up toothpaste with a free, extra-firm bristled toothbrush; a spool of "Jackson and Jackson" dental floss; a bar of Lux soap; and a beach towel that said "Fisherman's Friend," with a cartoon depicting a naked-from-the-waist-down fisherman getting a blow job underwater from a fugu. I also picked up two tires and tubes for Sweet Thunder; two tins of salted cashews; a box of toffee popcorn; a can of Wyler's

"Limited Edition" cola-flavored drink powder; a couple of bungee cords, just in case; and a large backpack to carry it all in. I offloaded the cart's contents onto the conveyor.

"Cash or credit?"

"Credit."

Goulet merely glanced at the items going by and punched in what seemed to be arbitrary prices.

"Ma'am? I was wondering. Can you recommend a decent restaurant nearby? Nothing fancy, just diner food; eggs, bacon."

"Open or closed?"

"Open would be better."

"The Crow's Nest, up the road."

"Thank you." She charged me only a buck and a half for the toothpaste and brush. I was curious. "One other thing, if you don't mind, ma'am. Do you know Opal Cove Road, just back a way?"

"I live on Tide Pool."

"I don't know it."

"It's one street over. Lived there my whole life."

"So if anyone could answer my question, it would be you. How far is Opal Cove Road from where we are right now?"

"Six-tenths of a mile. On the nose."

Get the fuck out of here. I had biked only slightly more than half a mile. I felt like I'd just failed a cardiologist-sanctioned all-day stress test.

My pathetic, defining possessions were having an orgy at the end of the moving conveyor. Goulet and I were the only people in the store. It didn't matter. She fixed a fluorescent orange PAID sticker to each of the bicycle tires. Three days earlier, Jocelyn said she'd love me for the rest of my life if I let her.

"Do you sell medicine cabinets? The ones with mirrors for doors?"

"In kitchens and baths. Left at the commodes."

"What do those go for?"

"Thirty-six ninety-nine or forty-two ninety-nine."

"Do you have one that's thirty dollars?"

Goulet shook her head.

"Okay. Ring me up one of the thirty-six ninety-nine jobs."

A COUPLE OF days after the Richie and Josie incident, I saw Jocelyn buying a newspaper and cigarettes at Ozzie's Tobacco Shop on Pleasant Street. She was wearing a pink tank top and olive-green painter's pants. Her toenails matched her shirt. I stayed out of sight behind a divider of greeting cards. When she started for the register I came out of hiding and followed her. I was shaking. I didn't know what I was going to say or what she'd think of me for living with Richie. That whole "The friend of the enemy of my friend is my enemy" thing can be powerful. I stood behind her in line. She turned when I coughed.

"Hey, how's it going?" I asked.

"Fine. You?"

I acted like a guy whose car is in the shop again. "Oh, you know."

"I hear you," she said. She asked Ozzie for a pack of Marlboro Lights. He put the smokes on the counter. "Oh, I'm sorry. I meant soft pack, not box. Thank you," she said sweetly.

I went for it. "Isn't it weird how you have to have the right kind of pack? I mean, are Marlboros in a soft pack better than Marlboros in a box?"

"Not better," Jocelyn said. "Better for you."

"Ah, so that's it."

"Keep it low. It's an industry secret."

"Huh. And to think all these years . . ."

"Same thing with Coke. A bottle's better than a can."

"Really?"

"Yup." She pocketed her change and headed for the door.

I threw a twenty at Ozzie. "Coke or Pepsi?" I called after Jocelyn.

"Give me a break. Coke. Canada Dry or Schweppes?"

"Canada Dry, hands down. Canada or America?"

"Canada," Jocelyn said. Ozzie didn't know what the fuck was going on.

"Canada? You must be out of your mind," I said. "Canada's practically communist."

"Oh, brother, you're not one of those, are you?"

"I don't think so. How do you tell?"

"You can never really tell, can you?"

"I can sometimes."

"Well, lucky you." She folded her paper under her arm. "Be good." She stepped out onto the sidewalk.

"Hang on a second. Aren't you going to have one of those smokes?"

"I plan on having all of them." She was quick and she knew it. I loved both of those things about her.

"I meant now, while they're still fresh."

"I'm in a rush."

"Come on. What are you going to say on your deathbed: I should have rushed around more?" Ozzie took his time with my change. "What's one little smoke?" Jocelyn smiled. I watched her as she waited for me on the sidewalk. A dark blue station wagon parked in front of Ozzie's appeared greenish, tinted by a dusting of pollen. By noon the air would be oppressively hot and humid. I knew the next thing I had to do was throw my good friend Richie under the bus.

"I still can't believe what happened with my roommate and your friend."

Jocelyn rubbed her irritated eyes. "He's a real winner. A keeper."

"I know. I feel bad about it."

"It's not your fault."

"I thought you'd think because I live with him that I—"

"I don't." She rubbed her eyes more vigorously.

"Are you okay?"

"Allergies." She sounded like she just got whacked with a wicked cold.

"That sucks."

"It does. I cannot wait to get the fuck out of here."

"You going somewhere?"

"New York."

"To visit?"

"To live."

I felt a sting. "Cool," I said. "When?"

"Middle of August."

"That's only a month away."

"Less. Three weeks and some change."

"You going for good?"

"Who knows?" Her eyes were red-raw. She tried blinking some relief into them. "People are going to think you made me cry."

TWO NIGHTS LATER Jocelyn and I were sharing a smoke on the bench in front of the Amherst Post Office. I had less than a month to talk her out of moving.

"How could you even think of moving? You just met me."

"Please. New York is crawling with guys singler than you."

"That's not even a real word."

"Yes it is. So is *wealthier*. New York is crawling with men singler and wealthier than you."

"I knew it. A gold digger."

"That's me: in it for the money. Like Gandhi."

"All the guys in New York are junkies," I said. "I read in the *Times* the other day—"

"The New York Times?"

"That every year, thousands of people get hep C just from riding the New York subway."

"Oh, they do, do they? I mustn't have read the paper that day." She was entertained. She had a smile that even she couldn't stop once it started. "What day was that?"

"And the promise of hep C is what they use to attract tourists."

"I see."

"Hep C and the possibility of getting spermed on by homeless guys."

"Eww. Fun is fun, but now you're just being sick."

"Come on," I said. "Tell me with a straight face that you didn't think that was funny."

"It wasn't funny."

"Bullshit. You're laughing."

"I'm laughing now, at the ridiculousness of this little . . . I don't even know what to call it . . . this little dance."

"Don't change the subject. I know you thought it was funny."

"Oh, so you can tell what I'm thinking?"

"Yes."

"What am I thinking?"

I rubbed her temples. "You're thinking, Moving to New York is a mistake. An el giganto mistake."

She slapped my hands from her head. "Have you ever been to New York?"

"Come on. Have I ever been to New York."

"When?"

"Recently."

"Recently, my fucking ass." She laughed. "You know dick about New York."

"Hey, listen here, toilet mouth. I find your language patently offensive."

"You should talk."

"Yes, I should. And I will. If anyone knows New York, it's me."

The last time I'd been to New York City was on a high school trip. I fucking hated it, not because New York blew per se, but it really brought out the more sophisticated urban asshole in some of the suburban assholes I went to school with.

"Is that so?" Jocelyn asked. "Mr. Zagat's. Mr. Hepatic. Mr. Homeless Spermer."

At that moment I definitely wanted to partake in frequent and varied sex acts with her. But way more than that, I just wanted to be around her. It's corny as fuck but true: If someone had told me I could freeze any minute and spend the rest of my life in it, I would have picked Jocelyn and me sitting on that bench in front of the Amherst Post Office. But who the fuck has the power to grant that kind of perpetual happiness? And if they did have it, why would they wield it on my behalf?

"I know there's nothing for you in New York," I said.

"And Amherst is what, the world capital of culture and opportunity?"

"It is." I flung open my arms like Mary Tyler Moore at the end of the opening credits. "Everything you need— and I don't mean some slick job or material shit, but the important stuff—is all right here."

"Really? Like what kind of important stuff?"

"The important stuff. Hey, are you hungry? I'm fucking starving. Want to split a foo yung at Hunan the Barbarian's?"

"You know what I think?" she asked. "I think you love distraction."

"Did you say something?"

She was free with her hands. She punched me in the stomach.

"Someone help me, please!" I called out. She hit me again, but harder. "I'd puke right now, but I'm so hungry, there's nothing in my stomach to puke." I faked a retch.

"You love distraction. Maybe more than anybody I've ever met."

"I told you I was different."

"You might be." She kissed me first. It took about five seconds before we were officially mashing in public. If I had been a mere witness to it, I would have hurled at our feet.

PAMELA'S SUBURBAN—with winterized boat still in tow—was parked in front of the house. I could see the back of James's head behind the wheel. I coasted to a stop on the driver's side. His window was open a crack, and he was talking on the phone, smoking. When he saw me, he rolled the window down to halfway, and smoke poured over the outside of it like water over a falls.

"Just the prick I want to see," he said. "No, not you—my brother-in-law. You, Teddy, are the prick I never want to see." James would probably always call me his brother-in-law, like he was divorcing only my sister and not me. "I'll be there in a few. Yeah, we're all set. Yes. Yes. Yes, Teddy," he said, agitated. "No. No, I have two full rolls in my truck as we speak. No, twenty-fives. It's plenty. Trust me. Because I've been doing this job since I was seventeen's how I know." He pulled the phone away from his ear and looked at me in disbelief. "How about if it isn't enough, I drive back to Orleans and get another roll and finish up alone?" The last proviso seemed to satisfy Teddy. James listened.

I sat there on the bike—on hold. I looked in the back of the Suburban to catch a glimpse of whatever kind of rolls James was sure would be enough for whatever job they were talking about. Roy was falling in and out of sleep, strapped into a car seat directly behind the front passenger seat. His head kept drooping forward, and he'd snap it upright, doze back to sleep, and so on.

"I just have to drop my kid off," James said. "I don't know, fifteen minutes." Then he hung up. "Fuck me," he said to the gods.

"What's up?" I said.

"The fucking guy—" He stopped himself when he saw me and the bike. "How you holding up?"

"Eh, you know."

"That's a nice ride you got there. Reminds me of my buddy Dogshit." James had a friend who actually answered to the name Dogshit. When Dogshit was a teenager he passed out at the wheel and cracked his two upper incisors. He never got them fixed, and they turned brown, like stubborn leaves that refused to fall. "You know Dogshit," James said, pulling at the outer corners of his eyes because Dogshit's mother was Korean.

I'd met him a few times. I called him David at first, and he looked at me like I had two heads, both filled with teeth more fucked up than his own.

"They busted him for DUI, and he wasn't even driving. He was parked." James found his recollection of the story entertaining. "He had to get back and forth to the boatyard on a friggin' ten-speed. You know, with the handlebars?" He traced the outlines of ram's horns. "Funny as all fuck, Dogshit pulling up all out of breath and he's pissed off, bitching to himself." James tapped his front tooth. "Nobody would give him a lift—I swear to Christ—just so we could watch him ride up in the mornings . . ." James trailed off, quieted by his own take on nostalgia. "He's a good shit, though, Dogshit."

"At least it's exercise." I pulled the front end of Sweet Thunder up into a stationary wheelie position. The tire knocked the driver's-side mirror out of whack.

"Hey, easy, easy." James readjusted the mirror. "Yo, what's this coming up behind us?" I turned around a lot more conspicuously than I would have had I known he was talking about Marie and not an El Camino or a Harley. She was wearing the same Kelly green track jacket. I was embarrassed because she had to think we were gawking at her. She turned her eyes to the ground. I spun back around and leaned forward with my forearms on the handlebars.

"Jesus," I said under my breath, "I thought you were talking about a car."

"Cars, women, whatever, they all like to be looked at." James and I pretended not to notice her as she walked past the Suburban. She was carrying a brown paper bag large enough for a six-pack and maybe a fifth of something. She drew the package closer to her breast. "Weird," I said when she was well out of earshot.

"You got that right."

"No, she bummed a beer and a smoke off me the other night," I whispered.

"Get the fuck out of here," James said.

"I'm serious. I was sitting right there, and she was walking by, just like that."

"No shit."

I nodded.

"What did you guys talk about?"

"Nothing. She skulled the beer in like two seconds, and that was it."

"Interesting," said James. "You must have made some first impression."

"Or she doesn't remember." I drank from my thumb. "Seems to me like she has a bit of a battle with a bottle, if you know what I'm talking about."

"It's fucking Cape Cod for chrissake," James said. "I'd still like to throw a fuck into that." I didn't second that emotion. James shot a look at me. "What, you wouldn't?"

"I don't know."

"Trust me, if you saw her in a bikini you'd know. Meat on her bones. Nice shitter. Tattoos everywhere. It's hot." He inhaled through his clenched teeth. "I'm into that Elvira thing. Not for anything serious, but a couple hours, no strings attached? Just tell me where to be." James could talk a good game, but to be honest, I didn't know how much of a follow-through guy he was. Then again, he must have followed through with enough of the wrong shit for my sister to want to divorce him. Pamela tried confiding in me when they were first having problems, but I told her I was too screwed up over Jocelyn to be of any use to her. After that, I'd ask her perfunctorily how things were going. She'd say "Same," "Worse," or "Better" if she said anything at all. "Okay," I said to James. "If this woman asked you to go—right this minute—you would?"

"And you'd watch Roy?"

"Sure, whatever."

James consulted his watch and smiled. "In a New York minute."

"Not me. I couldn't do that, especially now."

"Well, it's a mute point, isn't it? I don't see her coming back for you anyway." He thought I was judging him when in fact I was judging myself.

"What I meant was, the less I know someone, the worse the whole thing is for me. You're a free man—"

"Almost."

"I don't care who you fuck around with." I really didn't.

James understood. He handed me the Suburban's glowing cigarette lighter as a peace offering. He let his sensitive side show. "Do you have trouble hoisting?"

"Fuck no."

"Don't get worked up. I'm just asking." He ticked my

potential impotence off his checklist. He wiggled his pinkie. "Do you have a tiny pecker?"

"Huh?"

"That's not your fault, either. It's not like you chose it. You get the dick you're born with." He went on to paraphrase from his rickety cosmology. "Look, you're a decent guy from what I know of you. And you're not the ugliest motherfucker out there. A little shaggy-looking, maybe, but chicks might mistake that for your style. So if you think you have to lay a bunch of groundwork before you can lay pipe, you've got to have some kind of dick issue. Or—and this is a tougher nut to crack"—he pointed the pinkie at me—"you think you have a dick issue."

I watched Marie disappear. "I'm as average as the next guy."

"Well, there you go."

Roy let out a single cry, then smiled when he saw his old man's big face looking back at him.

"Wook who woke up," James said, his eyes wide with fake surprise. Adults—especially big, hairy men—talking like babies creeps me out. Roy was beaming.

"God, he looks so much like Pamela," I said.

"Everybody says that. I don't see it."

"He looks like you, too. But he looks a lot like her."

"He's the spitting image of my old man," James said. He was still admiring Roy when he shot me a look out of the corner of his eye. "Hey, I need to ask you a favor."

"What is it?" I couldn't imagine what someone in my position could do for anyone short of maybe elevate their head until the ambulance arrived.

"This big emergency repair's getting towed in from P-town." James checked his watch again. "Fuck, it's probably there already. Some rich fruits who want it done yesterday and are willing to pay through the ass." He let the concept of big-money-to-be-made spin in the air.

"And?"

"I was wondering if you could watch Roy for a few hours."

Giving my undivided care and attention to a leaky need machine was among the least appealing of my options. "For real?"

"Honest to God." He pulled a silver crucifix from under his shirt and kissed it.

"Can't Pamela?"

"I don't know. I didn't ask her."

"Why not?"

"Because." He was reluctant to show his hand.

Roy and I were basically strangers to each other. "Wouldn't he be better off with her?"

"Of course he would, but if I ask her, it'll look like I can't hold up my end of the bargain." He hardened like a quick-set epoxy. "And I don't want to give her any friggin' reason not to let me have my time with him."

"I don't think she'd do something like that."

"Oh, no?" He was dying for me to dare him.

"You know what? I don't want to know."

"No, you don't. Believe me. There's a lot of shit you wouldn't think she'd do." He lightened up when it dawned on him I wasn't Dogshit. "Seriously, the kid's a breeze. And what the fuck, it's only for a couple hours."

I looked at Roy. He was trying to convince a lime green Nerf football bigger than his face that it could fit in his mouth. When I didn't jump at the chance to be his mother for the day, James pulled out the guilt gun.

"Plus, one hand washes the other, right?" He forced my eyes with his own toward the ranch house I was staying in free of charge. He was right about one hand washing the other, but I still thought he was a prick for saying it and cashing in so soon.

"Sure. I'll take him for a while."

"See, kid? I told you he'd do it." James clapped his hands, then reached back and tickled Roy's stomach. He laughed so hard he got the hiccups.

I WAS SITTING on the back porch in the cool early-September night. The phone was stretched as far as it would go through the back door. Jocelyn's call was already over an hour and a half late. It was the fourth week into our long-distance relationship. I missed her a lot. When she'd called me from work earlier in the day, she still wasn't sure if she'd be able to get away from New York for the weekend. I pressed her hard to come up to Amherst. She said she really wanted to, but she was trying to make a good impression at *Redbook*. She was told on the q.t. by her internship supervisor there that a junior associate editor position might be opening up in the next few months. I would have made the trip to see her, but it was back-to-school weekend, and Lello's directive to the entire waitstaff had come down weeks earlier: Don't even ask for the time off. Richie said he was going to put in for the weekend off anyway, just to fuck with Lello.

A couple guys were moving into the apartment below ours. One was named Bri, the other Kev. They hadn't seen each other all summer. I could tell they were students, and this was their first off-campus place, because moving apartments is like putting your fucking life on trial. Bri and Kev sounded too happy.

"Kev, check out this sweet lamp I scored." Bri couldn't wait. He dug into a box right there in the driveway.

"Awesome," Kev said. " 'My goodness, my Guinness.' "

The telephone finally rang.

"Hello."

"How's your hemorrhoid?" Richie asked.

"Fucking swell."

"That's great news, but it's not why I called."

"What the fuck do you want?"

"What's the rush?"

"I'm expecting a call."

Richie made the sound of a whip cracking.

"Nice," I said. "What the fuck do you want?"

"I was just calling to tell you, asshole, that the Grifters and Shelby Foote are on *Letterman* tonight."

"No shit?"

"Yes shit. But the wop says he's going to seat people until the bitter fucking end. There's no way I'll be able to get to the Wacky Paki Packie before eleven." (The liquor store around the corner from our place was called Ravi's Package Store. Ravi himself once inquired of Jocelyn while she was buying smokes if she'd "care to accompany" him to see *Pulp Fiction*.)

"So you want me to go?"

"I know, it's a ten-fucking-foot death march from our door, and you'll only have two hours for your phone call instead of the usual, but can you help a buddy out?"

"Sorry, shit smear, I can't promise anything." (Translation: Consider it done.)

"Don't be a dick hole." (Translation: Thanks.)

The song "Unbelievable" by EMF rose through the porch floor. A body ascending the stairs divided the mothy yellow porch light. It was Kev. He saw that I was on the phone and stopped before completing the flight. I got rid of Richie. Kev was chubby, with a red crew cut and a freckled baby face. He was wearing flip-flops, green droopy basketball shorts, and a white UMASS CO-ED NAKED HOOPS shirt. He was probably about nineteen. Just looking at him made me feel ancient. We introduced ourselves. He seemed too pleased to meet me.

"We're moving in downstairs."

I had no desire to learn any more about him. "Oh, very cool."

"Seems like an awesome old house." He patted the clapboards like they were the hindquarters of a trusty steed.

"It's not bad."

Kev cut to the chase. "I don't mean to be a mooch neighbor, but you think you could give us a hand for like—no kidding—two seconds?"

Fuck me, I thought. Another fucking favor. I should have hidden inside with the lights out, like I do on Halloween.

"We got this L-shaped sofa, and it would be awesome if we can get it in without taking it apart in the dark."

"I'd help you out, man, but I'm expecting a call I can't miss."

"Two seconds, I swear. Then it's nothing but social calls for the rest of the lease." I said nothing. "Two seconds. Seriously. It would really save us a lot of time."

"Okay," I groaned. A comet tail of orange embers trailed my cigarette as it sailed over the porch railing.

"Thanks, bro. Seriously." He slapped me on the arm.

"Let's just do it."

Bri was waiting for us in the back of a U-Haul trailer. He shined a flashlight in my face. "Howdy, neighbor," he said.

Kev added a *y* to my name when he introduced us. I let it go. "He's expecting a call, so let's get this bad boy inside." He suggested Bri push from the inside, he pull the heavy end, and I support the middle as it came off the trailer.

"Sounds like a plan," I said, like J Mascis from his tune "Green Mind." It went over their heads.

"And lift with your legs, bro."

We were just getting into position when the phone rang. I was already three steps in the other direction when Kev or Brian said, "I think that's your call."

ON FRIDAY MORNING I took the ten-mile bus trip from Amherst to Northampton. I'd seen a fountain pen I wanted to buy for Jocelyn in an antique store on Market Street. The store smelled like the inside of a canvas bag my dead grandmother stored her retired shoes and hats in. The pen was a 1930s stainless-steel job. I figured if Jocelyn was going to work in the ink industry she ought to have a decent pen. The guy wanted fifty bucks for it. I entered the shop prepared. I'd strategically planted a hodgepodge of bills equaling forty-one dollars in my front pocket. It didn't make a fuck of a bit of difference how much money I had.

"Oooh, I'm sorry, but that pen sold." The guy looked like Richard Burton's homelier older brother.

"You're joking."

"Oh, no. A Parker like that doesn't stay put long in my shop."

"Damn. It was going to be a gift."

"What a shame. That would have been a lovely gift." At first I thought he was trying to break my stones, but he wasn't. He simply couldn't contain his feelings when it came to things of quality. "You know, that was not the only lovely pen I have." He laid out four others on the glass counter. Two of them were horrible. They looked like they were made out of what's swept up after someone shatters a Fabergé egg.

I pointed at the other two. "The simpler ones are more her style."

"Of course they are." He moved the gaudy offenders out of the spotlight. He started to give me the rundown.

I interrupted him. "How much?"

"Okay, then, the black Waterman is seventy-five, and the turquoise Parker is one hundred twenty-five."

"That's a little more than I wanted to spend."

"I see."

"How much are the other ones?"

"Those would be a good deal more, wouldn't they." He didn't even try to up-sell me. I picked up the Waterman and looked it over.

"This one is seventy-five?"

He nodded.

I removed the cap and touched the tip. "What do I have to do to put you behind the wheel of this pen?" I said like a southern used-car salesman.

"Nothing. A pen like this sells itself. It really does."

"Seventy-five bucks, huh?"

"Plus tax."

"Is there any wiggle room there?"

"I beg your pardon?"

"Would you take less than seventy-five?"

"I'm sorry. It's a consignment piece. I'm not authorized to go any lower." He took off his reading glasses and let them hang from their chain. "I could contact the owner and ask if that's his absolute lowest price."

"That would be fantastic."

"If he wasn't in Europe on a buying trip. Can you wait until next week?"

"I can't. It's for my girlfriend. She's only here for the weekend."

"I see. I see."

"Seventy-five dollars, huh?"

"Mmm."

I stroked the glossy black Waterman. "It is a beautiful pen."

"If I may?" He took the pen from me. "The giver of such a wonderful gift as this is never far from the heart of the receiver. I like to believe that words written with this lovely piece once bound two people together, just as they will again. That's what beautiful things do."

Give me a fucking break. "Do you take Visa?"

He smiled.

I took the bus back to Amherst and looked at the pen a few times along the way. Jocelyn was going to freak—in a good way—when I gave it to her. It was the most expensive gift I'd given to a girlfriend. I got off in Amherst Center and walked to Stop & Shop. I bought her a quart of fruit salad, some soymilk, and a few Golden Delicious apples that I lovingly shined to a glossy French finish. The day had already cost me close to a hundred dollars I didn't have, but I didn't care. I couldn't wait to see her.

I went home, cranked the Pogues' *Rum, Sodomy & the Lash,* and proceeded to scour the bathroom from top to bottom. The record started skipping during the final chorus of "A Pair of Brown Eyes." I didn't feel like walking to the kitchen, so I stomped on the floor a bunch of times until the stylus hopped over the album's problem spot. I kneeled back down in front of the toilet, and resumed scrubbing. So help me God, there was a small, thin-stalked toadstool growing behind the porcelain base. It looked like the umbrella in a moldy mai tai. I picked it and saved it in a mug. Richie was crashing somewhere else for the weekend so that Jocelyn and I could be alone. I didn't even ask him. I put the mug on his dresser with a note that said, "Two guesses where this came from?"

JOCELYN STEPPED OFF the bus like Princess Grace. She always looked good, but since she had moved to New York she'd hit a new stride. She was wearing a matching khaki skirt and blazer and a pair of chocolate brown suede gloves. Her hair had a postflight Amelia Earhart thing going on. Her eyes were the same shade as David Bowie's green one. They looked happy and tired. I couldn't believe that within minutes she'd be telling me I was the thing her life had always been missing. We kissed on the sidewalk. I stepped back and looked at her.

"Jesus, you look amazing."

"So do you."

"No, you really look mint."

"Thanks." She threw out a hip, supermodel style. "That's what working for the big boys will do to you."

I rubbed her shoulders. "Then I'm all for it."

She stopped smiling. "Please, don't hate me for what I'm about to tell you."

My heart sunk. "What?"

"If I could have helped it, I would have."

"What?"

"I have to do a few hours of work while I'm here." She bit her lip. She looked like she was bracing herself for punishment.

"Jesus H. Christ, don't do that to me. I thought it was something bad."

She smiled. She liked that I was generous when it came to exploiting the entertainment value in my neuroses. "Something really bad? Like what, I want to break up with you?"

"No, that would be plain-old bad. I thought you meant really bad." I collapsed onto a bench, taking her with me. She put her head on my shoulder. "Something really bad like, 'Oh, by the way I have stage-six chlamydia.'"

"Eww."

"I know. That would be really bad."

"I haven't been with anyone else since I last got tested, so I must have contracted it from you."

"Well, I haven't been with anyone else, either." We continued with the tease, buzzing from the roundabout admissions that our monogamous relationship had so far survived the separation. "So who gave you chlamydia?"

"Miraculous Contraction?"

"I think not," I said. "Why would God pick a half-Jew instead of a thoroughbred?"

"Good point."

"Dirty toilet?"

"Highly unlikely," she said. "I only go at home. And you know how anal I am about cleaning."

"Anal?" I asked like she was offering. She elbowed me in the ribs. I thought some more. "You get hit with full-blown chlamydia, and I'm clean as a whistle? It just doesn't add up."

"How do you know you don't have it? You could be an asymptomatic carrier." She could joust with the best of me.

I took her face in my hands. "You"—I kissed her—"are"—I kissed her again—"a fucking genius."

She turned and spoke to a nonexistent third party. "Finally, somebody notices."

We picked up some Chinese food, went to my apartment, and fucked. I told her Richie was gone for the weekend. She put her clothes back on afterward, anyway. We then went into the living room and watched Richie's copy of *Lawrence of Arabia*. I was a little nervous because who knew what he'd taped over. I had asked him in advance.

"Dude," he said, "it was a brand-new tape when I taped it." He wouldn't fuck with me——not like that. But he might forget. I didn't want Jocelyn and me to be sitting there watching Omar Sharif galloping off to Aqaba and all of a sudden the scene cuts to three enormous Sing Sing prison guards power-banging a tiny, restrained Asian woman begging for more, only harder.

Jocelyn ate her fruit salad for dessert. I ate an entire pint of double chocolate ice cream.

"Great movie," I said, and killed the power on the VCR just as the end credits started rolling. Jocelyn agreed but didn't feel like discussing it any further. She kissed me and told me to wait there on the couch. She disappeared into my bedroom. I could hear her unzipping her suitcase. "What's going on in there?"

"It's a surprise," she said.

"I have one for you, too."

"You do?"

"Uh-huh."

"That's sweet."

"I hope you like it," I said.

"I hope you do, too." I squeegeed the inside of the ice cream container with my finger. "Okay," she called. "You can come in now."

She was standing in the middle of my cesspool room,

wearing a cream-colored, spaghetti-strap nightie. She looked like a silk purse sticking out of a sow's ass.

"Well?" she asked.

"Holy shit."

"Is that good?"

"Yes."

"Want to feel it? It's nice on the skin." She pulled the string hanging from the ceiling light. The room went navy blue. I slid my hands all over her. She was instantly into it. She pulled me down to the mattress.

"Wait," I said, "I want to give you your present."

"Uh-uh. Yours isn't through yet."

I knew that, unless a lightning bolt or his-and-her fatal heart attacks befell us, I'd be coming in, on, or near her within minutes. That's the best kind of knowledge there is.

THE NEXT MORNING I woke to Jocelyn kissing my face. I rolled away because my breath stunk.

"Get back here," she said.

"Let me go brush my teeth first. My mouth's gross."

"I don't care."

"I do."

"I kind of like it," she said.

"That's sick." I streaked to the bathroom. When I got back, Jocelyn was sitting up in bed, admiring her pen.

"That was so nice of you. I love it."

"I'm glad." I slipped back in at the foot of the bed and started kissing my way up her legs.

"I should get you a nice pen."

"I'm not really a nice-pen guy," I said from under the sheet. I opened her legs. "I like Papermates. Blue ones, black ones, red ones, it doesn't matter."

She shifted to accommodate me. "So, what you're saying is a pen is a pen is a pen?"

"Is a pen."

"I see. What about a new journal? Something leather-bound?"

"Kinky," I said. She squeezed my head between her thighs. I could hear the ocean. "I'm not a journal guy, either."

"You're not a journal guy?"

"Nope."

"I don't believe you. Everyone keeps some kind of journal."

"Not me." She sat up, taking her pussy with her.

"Well, what are all those?" She stripped the sheet off my head.

"What are what?"

"Those."

My bedside table was a yellow towel draped over two milk crates stacked one on the other. The bottom crate was packed with identical black-and-white-marbled notebooks.

"Those are some of my notebooks from college." Two of them actually were aborted journals.

"They sure look like journals."

"They're not."

Jocelyn wasn't sold. "Why do you keep your college notebooks? You don't strike me as a 'keep my old note-books' kind of guy."

"I don't know."

"And they're so close to your bed, I just figured they were your journals."

"They keep my table from moving."

"Curious," she said.

"Is it?"

"A little bit." I pulled her back down by the hips. "If you want, I can stop, and we can critique them together right now."

"No, that's okay. Finish what you're doing. I'll just go through your shit sometime when you're out."

"Fine. And I'll go through all of your shit."

"Isn't that what you're doing right now?" She laughed once at her own joke, like a Joan Collins character getting serviced by a pool boy. She steered me by the head as I skimmed the surface of her deep end. She got into it. "I mean it," she moaned. "You can read my journal, my diary, anything. I want us to know everything about each other."

I got anxious. I thought, I don't want to fucking read her journal, do I? Sure, I'm curious, but I don't want her poking around through my stuff. I can move them into my closet the next time she goes to the can. Too obvious. She'll notice they're gone, and then she'll never stop asking me questions. I can't get rid of them until she goes back to New York. Fine. I won't leave her alone long enough to do too much digging. That's what I'll do.

"Hey, Tiger," she said. "Easy does it."

I DIDN'T KNOW shit about taking care of kids.

"Don't worry about it," James said. "This is all you have to do: Push him up and down the street until he falls asleep. He should stay out cold for a couple hours."

"What if he doesn't?"

"He will. And when he wakes up, feed him right the fuck away or he'll go ballistic." James held a stack of three identical Tupperware containers on top of a foil-covered baking pan. "There's diced fruit in this one, and chopped chicken and carrots in this one. This one's all Cheerios and Wheat Chex and shit."

"What's in the big pan?" James gave it to me. It was still warm.

"I don't know. Pamela sent it for you."

I removed the foil. Pamela was a good cook. The pan held a lasagna with a large divot taken out of it. "Weird," I said. "She must have run out of noodles to make a whole one."

"That's my haulage fee," James said.

I laughed. "Your haulage fee."

James was in a rush. "Come on. I don't have time to fuck around."

"Fine."

"So, feed him a bunch of this." He handed me the Tup-perware containers.

"How much?"

"I don't know. Until he starts crying."

"That seems kind of cruel."

"Maybe, but it's the only way to be sure he's getting enough. He'll definitely piss himself and probably shit. You'll be able to tell because he makes 'this' face, and he'll stink. You know how to change a kid?"

"Can't it wait until you get back?"

"Don't be an asshole." He hung a mommy bag on my shoulder. "Everything's in here. And when you do change him, make sure you put enough of that aloe oatmeal oint-ment on him. His ass is sensitive. So is his weld."

"His weld?"

"Where your dick joins up with your bag." James pinched at his weld. At least he didn't pinch mine. "Suit him back up and you're home free."

"Then what?"

"I don't fucking know. Let him run around until I get back."

I asked James if it was cool if I swore in front of Roy.

"Don't fuck around," he said. "Your sister will have my

nuts on a stick." Pamela was a pretty easygoing person. But once you push her past her breaking point, you'd better head for the fucking hills.

ROY WAS NOT very good at walking. But he screamed whenever I picked him up and tried to help close the distance between him and the object of his capricious desire. In order to get him into the stroller, I tricked him into thinking the stroller was what he wanted. I lifted it by an umbrella-hook handle and dangled it like a SeaWorld herring in his line of sight.

"Roy? Look at this, Roy. Smooth," I stroked the seat invitingly. I was a good deceiver. He fell for it. He locked on. "Come on, kid. Get in." I set the stroller down on the driveway about ten feet from him, lit a cigarette, and killed some time watching him labor to get from A to B.

He was pretty cute. He was wearing green Wellington boots, baby Levi's, a black longshoreman's cap, and an Irish knit sweater under a miniature L.L. Bean tan hunter's coat. His outfit was worth many times my own. When he finally reached the stroller, he screamed with a delight that was so sincere, I was actually kind of grateful to him. I hadn't smiled and meant it since I got married.

JOCELYN AND I babysat for Roy one night after Christmas so that James and Pamela could go on a last-ditch date. We didn't really do anything with regards to care-taking because Roy was asleep when we got there, and he stayed asleep the whole time. Jocelyn was in a good mood in spite of the holidays. We curled up on the couch and watched *Masterpiece Theater: A Scandal in Bohemia*. Jocelyn checked on Roy a few times and reported that he was just fine. She sank back into her dent on the couch. I could tell she liked playing house.

James and Pamela came home tipsy, laughing and hanging all over each other. It looked like they had a chance. James fixed us all a quick cinnamon schnapps nightcap before bed. "Here's to burying last year," he said.

"I'm all for that," Pamela added.

"Here's to the future," Jocelyn said.

"It can't come soon enough," James said.

We all turned in for the night. Jocelyn and I made up the pullout couch in the TV room.

"I know I'll make a good mother someday."

She was waiting for me to say I'd make a good father. That wasn't going to happen. But the night had been going along nicely. There was no reason to mess it up then. I did the best I could. "No doubt."

She smiled.

TAKING CARE OF ROY behind Pamela's back felt wrong for a lot of reasons. First of all, I definitely did not want to get caught. I knew if Pamela found out she'd rip both James and me new assholes. I figured there wasn't much chance of her showing up out of the blue, though, because Plymouth was a good thirty miles from East Falmouth. And if James was supposed to be taking care of Roy, chances were good that Pamela was working or catching up on doing laundry or some other domestic shit. I also felt guilty for scheming with James of all people. It was like I'd signed on to be his star, blockbuster witness in the upcoming divorce proceedings. But I assuaged my guilt by noting that Roy, too, was my blood and he needed me. And wasn't it as much James's house as hers? I was also nervous something horrible would happen to Roy on my watch. I felt like Joel in *Risky Business* when he goes cruising in his old man's Porsche without permission. If I accidentally drove Roy off the end of a pier, there'd be no gold-hearted hookers to raise the bread to fix him up without my sister knowing about it.

ROY WAS SLEEPING minutes after I'd tricked him into the stroller. I pushed him up and down the length of Opal Cove Road about a hundred times. I watched the ocean come and go in the gaps between houses—on my right in one direction, and on my left in the other. Taking care of a kid was easy enough so far. I started zoning out, thinking about Jocelyn crying.

I don't know how long it took me to realize it was Roy who was whimpering. He had been taking the brunt of a growing wind, softening my way, like an icebreaker's prow.

"Fuck me, kid. I'm sorry." I crouched in front of him

and cradled his cheeks. They felt like two packages of thawing ground beef. His eyes were watering, and his face twisted ugly as he teetered on the edge of crying. "No, no. It's okay, Roy. I'll take you back. Don't cry." I stretched the sleeves of his sweater until his hands disappeared. Then I breathed warmth into the wool tubes. I pivoted the stroller in the direction of my sister's and added the sound of a racing car's screeching tires to the maneuver. Roy giggled.

"Want to go zoom, Roy? Want to go zoom? Zoom-a-zoooooooom!" I was baby-talking, and was prepared to continue doing so as long as it kept him from crying. I pushed the stroller with dangerous bursts of speed. Roy loved that so much that he bawled when I stopped to catch my breath. And then he wouldn't stop crying, no matter how fast we went. I crouched back down in front of him so that we were face-to-face.

"Please, don't cry," I pleaded to his empathetic side. "Please, buddy." He scratched my glasses off my face. He did it three times before I caught on to the game. He was a tough read because the things he wanted were so simple. I let him play with my glasses and walked back to my sister's blind.

I had a headache. I sat on the front steps with a beer and a smoke. Roy was on the lawn, losing a wrestling match with his football. Watching him for the afternoon took it out of me, and apparently he was an easy kid. He brought the football to me.

"You know what's really fucked up, kid? Getting married was my idea." I booted the ball to the other side of the yard so he could chase it down. "I know. Hard to believe, right?"

James honked as he drove up. "How's my sonny boy?" he called, rounding the Suburban's long beak. Roy started to giggle and tried to stand up. "Everything go smooth? No problems?"

"No problems," I said. James tossed Roy above his head and caught/swung him so that the kid's path traced a J that skimmed the ground. They both laughed. It made me nervous watching Roy's head jerk back on its pencil neck each time he reached the bottom of that J. I was ready for the ride to end.

"James, do you think——"

"Hang on. I have to piss like a friggin' Clydesdale." He set Roy—who clamored for more—down on the grass and blew by me, taking the porch three steps at a time. "You want to go get some clams?" he asked on the go. "My treat?" He sounded like a guy who'd just made a lot of money. "Big bowl of beef stew and a few pints of Guinness?" The toilet seat went up with such force, I could hear the chalky underside of the tank lid ring and grind against the tank's unglazed coping. His piss stream broke the calm of the pond with a proud, throaty roar. "What do you say?" The raising of his diaphragm caused the pitch of his leak to momentarily modulate to a higher key.

I waited for him to finish before answering. "Maybe

next time." I took a pull off my beer. Roy was still wondering where the party went. "I'd kind of like to be alone."

The toilet seat slammed down on the mug. James boomed back across the living room.

"I don't fucking blame you." Then, almost apologetically, "What do you think about watching the kid for me here and there?"

I WAS INTO MUSIC, so it was bound to come up at some point. When it did, Jocelyn told me, not every detail about it, but enough. There was a band from Boston called Fifi, and before Jocelyn and I met, she had a brief fling with the band's front man, Roger Lyon III. Fifi never got famous—not like Third Eye Blind famous—but the cool kids knew who they were.

When I asked Jocelyn what had happened, meaning why it ended between her and Lyon III, she downplayed it and said there was "nothing there." I asked her if there was nothing there for her or nothing there for him. She said for either of them, which was a load of crap. There had to be something there for one of them. People don't feel the same amount of nothing for each other at the same time. She told me, well, that's the way it was. After that, I took every opportunity to assassinate Roger Lyon III's character.

I was eating a bowl of Cap'n Crunch cereal without any milk. I had *Option* open to the cover story on Roger Lyon III. "This guy's a fucking ponce." And he was, which made hating him a breeze. The two-page, fish-eye-lens photo elongated his already model-quality features. He towered over Sunset Boulevard in a shearling overcoat-and-hat ensemble that must have been rated for twenty degrees below zero. Jocelyn had her back to me. She was trying to light one of the gas burners. "I wonder if he still gets college girls wasted after shows," I said.

Jocelyn didn't answer.

"What do you think? Still getting college girls wasted?"

"He didn't get me wasted. It was two Rolling Rocks." She remembered the brand. "Give me your cig."

"Hang on. Listen to this. And I quote: 'I have tapes and tapes full of songs that are so much better than *Genius IQ*, but I'm not sure if I'm into the whole "releasing thing" anymore. I'm really into collecting opals.' End quote. Collecting opals? What the fuck is that all about?"

Jocelyn plucked the smoke from my fingers and used it to light the burner. She was wearing the boxer-briefs I had taken off when we got into bed the night before. She did that a lot.

"Holy fuck, get a load of this Q-and-A."

Jocelyn sighed.

"And I quote:

" 'OPTION: Where did the band name Fifi come from?

"'ROGER LYON III: The poodle protagonist from Van der Vleet's novella.

"'O: Very cool.

"'RLIII: Yeah.'

"What a fucking asshole. I bet he likes rape jokes." Jocelyn finished my cigarette at the stove. She looked good in my underwear. The kettle rumbled above a blue flame, but was still minutes away from boiling. "I bet Van der Vleet doesn't even exist. I went to college—"

"Sort of—"

"And I've never heard of fucking Van der Vleet. Have you? I bet that asshole made the—"

"Please. Enough. You have nothing to worry about. You're the asshole I love."

I WAS JUST wrapping up my morning shower when I heard a key opening the front door. "Yo, it's me and Dogshit," James hollered.

"Give me a minute," I yelled. I could hear James giving Dogshit instructions as I got dressed.

"Where the fuck this medicine cabinet come from?"

I opened the bathroom door. A draft further chilled my wet feet. "You don't have one, so . . . It's for letting me crash."

James appeared in the doorway. The medicine cabinet box hung from his hand like a Kleenex. "Fuck that.

The listed price for this place does not include a medicine cabinet." He meant it. "I can use this, though."

"Whatever, man. It's yours." I put a sock on one foot while balancing on the other like a pelican. I could hear Dogshit revving the motor of a small electric tool.

"You want all three of these, Jimmy?" he asked.

"Yeah. And don't lose the screws. They're brass."

"What's he doing?" I asked.

"Taking down the sconces. Look, you're going to have to clear out of here for a few hours tomorrow. A real estate agent's showing the place from noon to three."

"No problem. I won't be here."

"And stuff all your shit in the back bedroom closet before you split."

"Will do."

"I don't want them thinking this is a crack house."

"They won't."

James let go of the medicine cabinet box and pressed down with both middle fingers on a door hinge pin that had risen nearly two inches out of position. It wouldn't budge. It upset him. "You got a hammer out there, 'shit?" he yelled.

"Nuh-uh."

"Whore," James said. "Run out to the truck and get me one."

"Eat me," Dogshit said.

James bit his bottom lip and grunted as he tried again to pop the pin back into position. It finally snapped into place with a loud, metallic click. "Fuck you," he said to the hinge. He swung the door back and forth a few times to bask in the beauty of a specimen in perfect working condition. "Why don't you come to lunch with me and Dogshit?"

"Is it that late already?"

I SAT IN THE BACK, next to Roy's empty baby seat. It was a given that Dogshit always rode shotgun. James controlled the radio. He went right for a local oldies station.

"What sconces?" Dogshit said like a gangster film thug who understands that he, if questioned by the cops, is to play dumb. His thick navy blue hooded sweatshirt was faded and covered with smears of hardened epoxy, fiberglass dust, and small wood slivers. He wore a pilly black-and-gold knit cap commemorating the Boston Bruins' 1988 Stanley Cup run. "I never seen no sconces."

"No shit," James said. "I can get seventy-five bucks for those."

"Minus my twenty percent," Dogshit said.

"You can have twenty percent of this." James lifted his crotch off the seat.

"Oh, you'd love that, wouldn't you?" Dogshit said, and slurped the air.

"Not as much as you."

"Hold up," Dogshit said. "This is a good tune." Neither James nor I knew it. "You kidding me? It's Mel Tormé."

"That's what I like about this station," James said. "They'll throw you a curveball. It's not just 'Respect' and 'Get Off My Fucking Cloud' all day. The oldies stations ruined Aretha Franklin for me." Dogshit shushed him. James turned it up. We all listened in silence.

I always thought of Mel Tormé as singing exclusively bouncy, shoo-bee-doo-bee-doo-wah numbers, but this one was doleful and so slow, it almost went backwards.

James pulled onto a winding wooded road that soon presented a decent ocean vista on our left. The road rose above sea level and briefly wound around a craggy out-cropping of rock. I looked down at the water and counted three staggered white stripes of breaking waves. The ocean absorbed all of the sun's component light except the bluest green, and melted seamlessly with the sky somewhere closer to England. My feet were still cold. I missed Jocelyn, even though she could suck the life out of me.

The song cross-faded into a commercial for East Falmouth's only authorized dealer of Dittler Aquatic machined stainless steel crankshafts, camshafts, and valve lifters.

"I don't buy it," James said.

"Buy what?" Dogshit was already taking it personally.

"The whole thing."

"What? You think Mel Tormé doesn't mean it?"

"I think Mel Tormé means it. You can tell. He's really

putting his dick into the song. It's the song itself." They had cigarettes going, like French cafe intellectuals.

"What's wrong with the song?" Dogshit asked.

"It's supposed to be about love, right?"

"You think? The word *love* is in the fucking title."

"Shut the fuck up." Dogshit turned and high-fived me. James started over. "It's about love, and how it lasts forever and all that shit. Well, maybe, but it's not all fucking and flowers like the tune says. It's a grind. It's a second, low-paying job." He reloaded. "Mel says he'd break his balls at work all day for the rest of his life just to be able to come home to what's-her-face—"

"Monique."

"Whatever. Maybe when you first start screwing you feel like that. But that shit goes. Get married and have a kid, Mel. We'll see how fast you race home after work." Our eyes met for an instant in the rearview mirror.

"Okay," Dogshit said. "But did you ever think—and I don't mean anything by it . . . I'm just saying . . . did you ever think that maybe what you and Pamela had wasn't love?"

"Listen to Mr. Fucking Romance Novel here. I was there, asshole. And for what—two-plus years, maybe— it was love."

"Fine." Dogshit let it go.

I started thinking about getting Jocelyn pregnant. We were in Ray's Pizza in SoHo—not for the actual conception, but when we found out. I was so anxious I couldn't

Joe Pernice

84

wait until we got back to Brooklyn for her to take the test. She didn't want to do it in Ray's Pizza, but I wore her down. She came out of the restroom looking too calm for it to be positive. I honestly thought I was off the hook until she formed a cross with her two index fingers. I made her say the words. Even then I didn't believe her. Did I want her to go dig the stick out of the trash? You're goddamn right I did. I grabbed her by the wrist when she got up. She told me to face the facts. I felt condemned to death. I said "Holy shit" about a hundred times. She told me to stop saying that. There was plenty of time to figure it out. Figure it out? What was there to figure out? The paisan behind the counter came over to our table and gave us free slices. Time to figure what out?

That night Jocelyn was especially worked up, which got me going. She said it was the hormones. She begged me to fuck her without protection. I went at her pretty hard. In my wildest, desperate dreams, I thought I might dislodge whatever it was clinging to the inside of her uterus. I resented her for getting us into this situation, though I was as much to blame, if not more. I made her come twice. I had to look away from her face or I wouldn't have lasted as long as I did. I pulled out at the last second. Afterward, she mopped herself with my Teenage Fanclub T-shirt. I didn't care. We fell asleep without talking.

The next morning she shook me awake. Her face was sapped of some color. She said she'd just miscarried. I sobered up. Was she sure? Definitely. Did she want me to call an ambulance? No, she just wanted to sleep. A drink of water? A cup of coffee? No, just sleep. Another blanket? Please, no more questions. She curled up like a fetal pig on the beige top sheet. I combed her scalp with my fingers. It looked like someone else's scalp. The sharp edges of the Brooklyn street noise were rounded over some by the apartment walls. Jocelyn drifted off. I sat up in bed, chewing my nails. I didn't exactly feel like I'd dodged a bullet. It was more like the bullet had passed through me without damaging any vital organs. The next time I might not be so lucky. I wondered how long I'd have to wait before I broke up with her.

"I'D JUST LIKE IT BETTER," James said, "if the guy who wrote the song wasn't trying to put one over me."

"You know that's Cole Porter you're talking about?"

"I don't care if it's Peter Fucking Frampton."

I CAME IN through the back door. Richie was sitting at the kitchen table, reading the *Valley Advocate*.

"Dude," he said, "guess who's playing the Metro?"

"GodheadSilo?" I asked excitedly.

"Even better. Frampton."

"Peter Frampton? Get the fuck out of here."

"I'm not shitting you. Playing with Bowie must have given him the touring bug."

"That is fucking awesome."

We absolutely had to go. We were big fans. We had four-tracked an acoustic medley of "Baby, I Love Your Way" into ELO's "It's a Living Thing." We were not being ironic. Richie and I both agreed that irony was for chumps, and that irony in music was the worst kind of irony. That was one of the things that bummed us out most about the Amherst music scene: every time you turned around there was a new band of little Ivy Leaguers with Cinderella or Quiet Riot tunes strategically placed in their über-intellectual math rock sets.

The first time we played an acoustic open mic night in town, Richie conjured his best Bill Hicks: "Nice fucking irony-on T-shirt," he said to some dude wearing a new Kiss T-shirt. "There's absolutely zero room for ironicomic relief in music. 'Cum On Feel The Noize' motherfuckers. Come on and suck my ass. Fucking palate cleansers. Fucking melon balls. Fuck off." He tapped the mic. "Is this thing on?"

"Unfortunately," someone in the lean audience said.

Richie carried on. "In case you never noticed—which you probably haven't—this next tune is a great fucking song." Then we broke into a cover of "Chevy Van" by Sammy Johns.

"Dude," Richie said, "Frampton. I'm putting in tomorrow for the night off."

"Same here."

"Right the fuck on," he said. We shook hands like Romans, grabbing each other's forearm.

"When's the gig?" I asked.

"Twenty-seventh. It's a Thursday."

I winced. "This month?"

"Yes, why?"

"I can't go."

"What do you mean, you can't go?"

"I can't go. That's Jocelyn's birthday."

"So what?"

"So it's her birthday. I mean, I'm going to have to hang out with her."

"You make plans yet?"

"No, but—"

"So take her to Tanglewood for the weekend. There's got to be a Marsalis or some shit like that playing."

"She won't go for that."

"Make her go for it. Take her the next weekend, too. This is fucking Frampton."

I thought about it. "There's no way we're ever going to get another chance to see him, is there?"

"It's once in a lifetime."

"Fine. Get me a ticket."

I KNEW JOCELYN was going to shit a golden brick. We were standing on a footbridge in Prospect Park. The water was a turbid amusement-park green.

"I did something," I said. "And I don't want you to be upset about it."

She looked worried. "Well, since you put it that way . . ."

I told her my plan.

She was hurt. "But that's my birthday."

"I know, but we can celebrate it early, or late, or both."

"It's not the same."

"Why?" I asked like she was being childish.

She got a little pissy. "Because it isn't, that's why."

I dismissed her by acting like I couldn't relate to such a silly belief. "That's just"—I shook my head—"Jesus, I don't know."

"It's a real fucking shame if you can't understand what's so fucked up about making plans with your friend on your girlfriend's birthday."

I backpedaled. "Of course I can understand, I just don't—"

"Don't what? Give a shit?"

Two teenagers were crossing the bridge on skateboards. I was going to wait until they passed before continuing, but Jocelyn couldn't wait: "You could have at least talked to me about it before making other plans."

One kid nudged the other to make certain he wasn't missing any of the fireworks. They stopped close by and pretended to be looking over the other side of the bridge.

"You didn't even think to come and talk to me first. And I'm supposed to be your girlfriend."

"And what would you have said if I had asked you?"

"I don't know," she said.

"I do. Believe me."

"Don't be a dick."

I changed courses. "Look, this is once in a lifetime."

"And what am I? What the fuck am I?"

"You are, too. But Frampton's never coming around again. Ever. It's a big deal."

"And I'm not?"

"Of course, but—"

"But you'd rather see Peter Frampton with Richie."

The skateboard kids were enjoying the show. They were cramping my style. "Can we talk about this at your place?"

"No. I want to talk about it now."

I lowered my voice, but made up for the decrease in volume with a boost in intensity. "Fine. Let's fucking talk about it right here. If you postponed my birthday celebration—which I don't even fucking want, by the way—if you postponed my birthday because something like Frampton came up, I wouldn't have a problem with that. I wouldn't. I just . . ." I trailed off.

"Are you finished?"

"For now."

"Fine. First of all, you're so full of shit about not having a problem with it. And secondly, I do have a problem with it. That alone should be enough of a reason for you."

"I'm full of shit? Okay, when my birthday comes around, try me, and see what I say."

"I don't want to try you. I just wanted to spend my birthday with you. I don't have parents or a sister calling me all the time to tell me how fucking great I am."

"And that's my fault?"

"No, but—"

"You make it sound like it is."

"It's your fault when you treat me like I'm someone you're just fucking. I mean, you didn't even ask me if I wanted to go."

"To Frampton?"

"Yes, to Frampton."

"And you'd go?"

"Not with you and Richie."

"Why? It's not like we have to stand with him."

"Oh, yeah, right. What are you going to do, tell him to keep away from us?"

"Yes."

"That's a great idea. Then he'll think I'm a royal fucking bitch."

"Well, what's he going to think when I go back and tell him to sell my ticket because I can't go?"

She gave me a look like she genuinely hated me. "He'll think whatever you tell him."

"You know what? Maybe this isn't a good idea."

"What isn't?"

"This."

DOGSHIT'S GIRLFRIEND, CARRIE, was a clinician's assistant at an HMO in Cotuit. On Wednesdays she didn't leave for work until half past one.

"Swing me by hers after lunch, Jimmy," Dogshit said while shaking a bottle of hot sauce. "She said if she's still there, she'll give me a quick smoker."

"What about work?" James had a mouth full of egg salad sandwich.

"What about it?" Dogshit pointed the hot sauce at me. "You have to take him home, right?"

"So."

"So you'll be going right by her place in both friggin' directions. Zip-zip."

"And how fucking long do you think it's going to take for me to drop him off?"

"Long enough. Trust me. I got chowder backed up to here." Dogshit touched an imaginary waterline on his forehead.

James stopped chewing. "Please. I'm trying to eat here. I don't need to picture that."

Dogshit laughed. "What can I say? I've been in dry-dock for a week."

"Okay, so you pop in three seconds. Aren't you going to have to pay her back?"

"Not this time. I gots me a credit." Dogshit stuck out

his fat tongue. It looked like an inverted seal hide curing in a cave of petrified guano. James took a bite of sandwich. "I swear to Christ, if you're not waiting for me in the driveway, I'm going right by. That's all I'm saying."

"Don't you worry. I'll be the sleepy one with the shit-eating grin."

"What the fuck else is new?"

Even Dogshit laughed.

CARRIE'S WHITE CHEVY Citation was parked in the driveway.

"Game on," Dogshit said. He stuck his hand in his pants. "Do I need a whore's bath first?" He raised the hand to James's face. James swatted it away.

"Get the fuck out of here."

We jettisoned Dogshit without coming to a complete stop. He flipped us the bird. I climbed into the front seat. James sighed. "At least someone's getting laid," He merged back onto Plymouth Street. He was flummoxed. "What I don't understand is how can someone like Carrie, who's so . . ."

"Normal?"

"And Dogshit's so . . . whatever, man."

"Someone for everyone, right?"

"At least for a little while."

James turned on the radio. A station I.D. segued into "That's How I Got to Memphis" by Tom T. Hall. I liked that song, but James groaned and turned the radio off without scanning for anything better. "Listen," he said, "I don't want you to get the wrong idea about what I was saying earlier." He could have been referencing any number of things.

"What are you talking about?"

"The stuff about the Mel Tormé tune."

"Right."

"I mean, Pamela's your sister and everything. And just because she and me got shit-canned, well, that doesn't mean, I don't know. I just don't want you to think I think she's a total bitch. She can act like one—they all can—but she's not one. You know what I mean?"

"I think so."

"It just didn't work out with us. That's all. And we're better off for killing it when we did instead of hanging around watching it rot. You follow me?"

"I can tell you don't hate each other."

"Hate? Jesus Christ. She's my only kid's mother. I'll always love her." I could feel him looking over at me, but I didn't face him. "And as far as Roy goes, shit. The little bastard runs me ragged, but I couldn't imagine the life I'd have without him. Just because I bitch a lot doesn't mean shit. The toughest thing about splitting up is not seeing Roy every day."

"But you get him half the week?"

"It's not enough. You think I like letting you watch him?" I was touched. It was like James had stripped out of his asshole suit right before my eyes. "I'd take a kid over a wife any day of the week," he said. "It's fucked up, I know. But having a kid changes you like that. You'll see."

"The fuck I will."

"What? You think you're never going to want a kid?"

"Never."

"We'll see. You're still young." He let it go at that.

"I got Jocelyn pregnant. That's as close as I ever want to get."

"She's not still pregnant, is she? Is that why you got married?"

"God, no." I told him the whole story.

"And she definitely didn't want it?"

"She said she didn't, but it was over so fast. Who knows if she would have changed her mind?"

"I did. I didn't want Roy at first, either."

"No?"

"Fuck no. But people change." Hearing that made me feel worse. James was insane over Roy.

"Maybe I would have changed. I just know there's no way I could have handled having a kid."

James thought about it. "I guess if both people don't want to have the kid, miscarriage is the way to go."

"It is, isn't it?"

"It's like having an abortion without having to have an abortion."

I shuddered. "I can't even imagine what going through that would have been like."

"It's a fucking nightmare. I've been through a couple of them."

"A couple?"

"Well, one, really. The second time, so help me God, we were pulling into the clinic lot—right into the spot they reserve for you—and she tells me she made the whole thing up. Just like that. 'I made the whole thing up.'"

"You're kidding?"

"Oh, no. I'm dead serious."

"Who was it?"

"Not your sister."

That was good to know. "God, you must have been floored."

"I didn't make me feel too good." He rolled his window down a crack. "After the first abortion I didn't doubt her when she said she was pregnant again."

"Same person?"

"Correct."

"Why'd she do it?"

"To get back at me."

"For what?"

"For fucking around on her with your sister." I knew Pamela and James's relationship was the surviving line segment of a love triangle, but as I'd understood it, Pamela had been there first. "It's was a shit maneuver, when you think about it," James said. "Her pretending she was pregnant."

THE BOURNE BRIDGE was ten miles away from East Falmouth. I wasn't going to do anything stupid when I got there. I just wanted to stand on it and think and watch the canal slide out to sea. Maybe get whacked by an epiphany. You always hear stories like that. Some successful yet empty-hearted commodities broker decides to give it all up and sculpt full-time while witnessing the sun sinking beyond the Grand Canyon. If something like that happened to me, or if some angel-in-training came down to guide me, like in *It's a Wonderful Life*, so be it.

When I was a kid, the suicide hotline signs posted at either end of the Bourne Bridge were sources of quality funning around for my family. My mother said my father and Pamela and I were bad for joking about desperate people, but she was saying it as much for herself. She always ended up laughing with us.

I was too hungry to bike the ten miles without eating first. I headed over to the Crow's Nest and stuffed my face. The Crow's Nest's patron-attracting hook was that it had once been the galley of an actual ship. But that was about a hundred years ago. Since then there had been numerous sloppy additions and upgrades. There was nothing except a wall of telltale photos and the unusual narrowness of the main dining room to hint at its original gig.

The *Nimitz* was the biggest one-stop-shopping break-

It Feels So Good When I Stop

fast on the menu. I ordered a chocolate malted shake on the side, and drank it right from the stainless steel cup. My waitress could have been a contender for Ms. Off-Season East Falmouth. I closed my eyes, and hers became the tight-pored voice of a girl half her age.

"Makes you think you'll never feel hungry again," she said.

She was absolutely right. I watched her wipe down the counters while Roger Whittaker sang "Durham Town." I pictured her and me getting an apartment together and living a life free from turbulence.

"Makes you think you'll never feel hungry again," I heard her say to a couple guys a few tables away. Turns out she had to say it. That was the Crow's Nest's slogan. It was printed on the back of her sweatshirt and others like it on sale at the register for $15.95. It figured she was pitching me. I know what it's like serving people for money and not from the goodness of your own heart. She wrote, "Thanks a bunch, Jeanine," and drew a smiley face at the bottom of my check. It was an insincere, tip-milking come-on.

I started thinking about a girl named Jeanine whom I'd had sex with a single, unhappy time. We were both sophomores at UMass. I was a much deeper shade of sexual green than she was.

I'd met UMass Jeanine a couple of times through our mutual friend Claire, but she was too hyper for me. And she had an overbite I just could not forgive. Claire was driving us back to Amherst after a long weekend in February. It was a rainy Presidents' Day, and already dark by the time we left Boston. Claire was a small, jittery girl with short, noticeably thinning hair. She dressed like a child. She always wore corduroys that were maroon or yellow or aqua. She downshifted her Dodge Omni into the gear designed for snow and never deviated from it or the right lane. Her bony ass squirmed on a folded towel she sat on for lift.

Traffic, shitty visibility, and the fact that I am a horribly nervous passenger made the Mass Turnpike a white-knuckle migraine maker. Claire kept the heat cranked because the defroster was fucked. When I wasn't obeying her short orders to wipe the windshield with a dedicated chamois, I was stabbing the phantom brake pedal on the passenger side. Claire stabbed the real brakes every time the spray plume from a passing truck drenched her windshield.

A George Michael EP cassette of five different mixes of the tune "I Want Your Sex" never left the tape player. When "Monogamy Mix" came around for the third time, I turned the power off. Claire was curt. She corrected me. She said it was her driving music. It relaxed her, okay?

For most of the drive I felt like I could be sick at any second. Not Jeanine. She said that since her bulimia was in remission, she refused to not see the positive in every-thing. I didn't buy it. She reminded me of an overly bub-bly suicide failure pretending to be over it.

I made a few comments about how a beer at the end of the drive was in order. Jeanine said she could really go for something with Midori in it. That was the extent of our flirting. I was wearing hemmed acid-wash jeans, a gray UMass sweatshirt, and white leather Reebok sneak-ers; in spite of all that, when we pulled up to her student apartment in Puffton Village, Jeanine asked me if I still wanted that beer.

We wound up on her Salvation Army sofa. One of the three seat cushions was gone; it broke the ice. We had to sit close. She read me her favorite passage from Sartre's *Nausea*—where the main dude almost drops dead from merely seeing a bloated scrap of paper in a puddle. Then she started shampooing me—both of us fully clothed—with beer right there on the couch. She kept saying she'd do anything I wanted. Anything. That all I had to do was tell her what I wanted her to do. She started kissing my throat. She'd put on too much Anaïs Anaïs during her last trip to the can. I could taste it. I asked her if she had any protection. She said if she got pregnant she'd just kill it.

I GAVE Crow's Nest Jeanine my standard 20 percent tip and left the restaurant. The sky was an electric-blue mono-chrome textile interrupted by Magritte-white crowns of cauliflower. It insisted I watch. I straddled Sweet Thunder in the lot and lit a smoke. I felt like getting laid.

"This is not a fucking pipe."

I started thinking about how the French phrase for giving someone head translates back to English as "to make the pipe." Jocelyn was fluent in both. I could be doing something as sexually arousing as spanking the bottom of a bunged-up toaster, and she'd poke her head in and ask, "Make the pipe?" If I took a rain check—which almost never happened—it was partly because there'd always be more where that came from. Jocelyn was of a different mind. She didn't take enough things for granted.

I finished my smoke, went back into the Crow's Nest, and jerked off into a urinal.

JOCELYN AND I woke from an afternoon nap and started fucking. She was on top of me. Her face always looked pained during sex. I didn't think anything out of the ordinary was up until she stopped mid-sprint and started to cry.

"What is it?"

"This," she said. "This." She opened her arms, presenting the moment and beyond.

"What about it?" She brushed the hair away from her eyes to make sure I could see a deathlike inevitability in them. "One of these times really is going to be the last time."

"Jesus Christ," I sighed.

"Well, it's true."

"And guess what? We're all going to die."

She fell onto her side. "I know. We are."

FROM WHEN I was about six until I started high school, my parents rented a house in the town of Dennis for two weeks most summers. When we were savvy enough to catch the pun, Pamela and I would crack up as my old man pointed out triumphantly upon approaching it, the sign that read Entering Dennis.

During one of the energy crisis summers—I must have been eight or nine—they had odd/even days. You could buy gasoline only on an odd day if your license plate ended in an odd number, and only on an even day if your plate ended in an even number. I don't remember if our Mercury Monarch was odd or even, but it was our day. My old man made an adventure out of it. He got me up at five to beat the rush, and it worked. We lined up at the Arco station behind a short queue. My father nudged me. "We—you and I—are very smart people." Arco had a sales promotion going back then. If you filled up, you got whichever free miniature Noah's Ark animal they were giving away that week. It didn't make sense to me, and I was only a kid. We were in the middle of an energy crunch. People were dying to overpay for gas. They didn't need a biblical myth to bring in the punters.

I was sitting on the sofa-sized front seat, feasting on leaded gasoline fumes. My old man stuffed his change into a pocket of his new Bermuda shorts as he walked back to the car. He tossed a pack of Hostess Donut Gems and a plastic animal onto my lap through the open window.

"It's a zebra," he said. "Next week's its mate." I couldn't care less. I'd just seen my dream purchase: A cluster of goatskin wineskins hung on an outdoor rack. Six dollars and ninety-five cents was a lot of cash.

"Well, it's your money," my old man said. When we got back to our rented cottage, my mother looked at the wineskin like it was still bloody. She told me to soak it in soapy water before I used it. After that, every drink tasted like Lemon Fresh Joy. It gave me headaches, so I stopped drinking out of it. I broached the subject of buying another one with my old man. This time he put his foot down.

SINCE OPENING IN 1949, Donnelly's Outfitters had been just over the Bourne Bridge into Cape Cod. We always stopped there either at the beginning or end of our family vacations. It was a tradition.

Donnelly's will have a wineskin.

The building was an army Quonset hut painted to look like a "Go west, young man" – era trading post. The anachronistic-by-design visage was accentuated by Precision Auto-Cad Fabricators, Inc., with which Donnelly's shared a chain-link fence. When I was a kid coming here to ride the go-karts and rummage through the shelves packed with cool shit, it really seemed like the place was out in the sticks. Like the person who'd buy the bear trap from above the faux fireplace might actually get some local intended use out of it.

I pulled on the locked door. The lights were on inside, but I couldn't see any people. The same sad man-sized mechanical flying fish hung on a wire fixed to an exposed ceiling rib. I knocked a few times. Nothing. I followed a mulch path around the side of the building to a side entrance. I could hear someone out back riding a go-kart. I followed the noise.

The lone go-kart darting around the track was piloted by the original Mr. Donnelly's son, Mr. Donnelly Jr. He must have been in his seventies. He looked like a dehydrated version of his younger self. His decimated white comb-over stood up like a ragged flap of dead skin. His knees were in his armpits. He was wearing a snowflake-patterned red cardigan I know was from Lands' End because I got the same one, but in blue, from my mother's sister Dee two Christmases earlier. Seeing Mr. Donnelly Jr. in that sweater helped me to further rest my case; it was not a sweater worn by a guy my age. Sure, Kurt Cobain made cardigans cool again, but his were beat to shit. I had the good sense to leave the tags on Aunt Dee's gift, that way I could get more fuck-off money from a used-clothes store in Amherst. Even so, I only got ten bucks for it. Dee lived way up in North Conway, New Hampshire, and she's dead now anyway, so no harm, no foul.

I moved through the chain-link corral that framed the crabgrass infield, the go-kart track, and a small prefab garage that looked new compared to everything else. The asphalt circuit was cracked and worn nearly silver. Skid marks pointed in unfathomable directions. The air smelled of salt, pine sap, and lawn mowers.

Mr. Donnelly Jr. sneered as he maneuvered the speeding go-kart through a tight chicane. He momentarily went up on two side wheels, then slammed down without even braking. The last time I'd driven a go-kart, I was in junior high, and it was around that very track. They didn't seem at all dangerous to me back then.

Mr. Donnelly Jr. noticed me leaning against the fence. He eased off the gas, as if capitulating to the hard reality that his victory at Le Mans was a mathematical impossibility. He raised his be-with-you-in-a-second finger and pulled out of sight into the garage. The engine went quiet off camera. He walked toward me. I felt kind of bad because he looked like he'd been having a good time, and, really, how many good times does a guy his age have left?

"Didn't think anyone was coming today." He was tall and thin. His kneecaps knocked like ball-peen hammerheads against the inside of his pants. His cheeks were bloodshot and stained with age spots. But it was a kind face. His hands looked kind, too, but you never know. They isolated a key on a large, crowded ring.

"Sorry to pull you away," I said.

"That's what we're here for, right?" He was the type of benevolent guy who says "It shows to go you" or, if you're a kid, pretends his thumb is your stolen nose. He looked out over the empty go-kart track. "I still love riding them, even after all this time." He didn't seem the slightest bit embarrassed by the fact that he wasn't talking about golf or bowling.

"I don't remember them going that fast."

"They don't usually. The one I was driving has no governor on the carburetor. Someone your size"—he looked me up and down—"could do thirty-five, forty easy. Give it a go? You don't have to open it up all the way if you don't want."

"No, thanks."

"Come on. Give it whirl."

"Maybe another time, thanks."

"Sure," he said. "Another time." I think he was slightly miffed because he got down to business without making any more small talk. He looked at me, then locked the gate behind him. As we walked back toward the store, I felt like I should offer something to fill the silence, like I owed him that much.

"I used to come here every summer with my family."

"Cape's a nice place."

"I mean right here." I pointed at the ground.

"Lots of people been through here." He bent over and picked up a flattened cardboard coffee cup that had blown onto his property.

Okay, fuck it, I thought. I don't want to talk, either.

Mr. Donnelly Jr. decided to forgive and forget: "Just down for a visit? Good time of year for it. All the loonies are gone."

"Sort of. I'm staying with family in East Falmouth."

"I like East Falmouth. East Falmouth, Falmouth, Barnstable—they're more real." He rubbed some salt of the earth between his thumb and fingers. "Real people. Know what I mean?"

"I think so."

"That's good." He laughed. "Because I don't know if I know what I mean." His teeth were neat, though not his own. We were friends again. He unlocked the side door and flung it open. The sleigh bells fixed to it chimed. The interior of the store—contents included—looked the same as it did when I was kid, only now I noticed an irrelevance that must have always been there. I overcame an urge to not go in.

"So, what is it I can do you for?"

I lied right to his face. "It's kind of silly, but I bought one of those goatskin wineskins here about twenty years ago—" He snapped his fingers and made a beeline to the correct shelf. "This what you're looking for?"

"That's it exactly." It came in a cellophane sleeve that

was brittle and yellow around the edges. The staple that sealed the package was rusted. Mr. Donnelly Jr. took it from my hand and brought it up to the counter. We both knew my buying it was a forgone conclusion.

"Anything else?" he asked.

"How many of those little Jameson's nips you got back there?"

"Let's see. One, two, three, four. Four."

"I'll take all of them."

It was a few days before Halloween. Mr. Donnelly Jr. looked at me like he'd just rung up my bag of apples, and I'd asked him to toss in a pack of razors.

I GOT BACK onto Route 28. People who had jobs were driving to their lunch spots. I stayed on the thin strip of right-unjustified pavement that separated the white line from a sand-and-scrub-brush shoulder. A couple times I had to stop to avoid veering off the road or into traffic. I wore the wineskin like a shoulder holster against my skin, concealed beneath my hooded sweatshirt and denim jacket.

I could see the Bourne Bridge in the distance. It was an arc of gray discipline rising from, then dipping back into, the mayhem of trees. It seemed out of place and was as arresting as the sudden appearance of a second, larger moon.

As I passed a dirt fire road on my right, the speed-trap cop parked in it gave me a choked-off blast of his siren. I stopped. He waved me over to his window. He was shaking his head like he was witnessing a weekend inventor about to test a prototype flying suit.

"What are you thinking?" he said. He was wearing a baseball type of cop hat and one of those black marksman's sweaters with the leather rifle-butt shoulder patches. The visible portion of his close-cropped blond hair screamed honorable discharge. He looked like the young leader of a Mormon paramilitary group.

"Nothing."

"Affirmative." The admitted purposelessness of what I was up to did not improve his opinion of me. I was guilty as fuck of being stupid. He looked at the bike and the four-day growth on my face and clothes. If I had been wearing the wineskin outside my jacket he would have run my license.

My license. I felt a jolt of raw nerve panic. I was sure I'd left it on the writing table at the Gramercy Park Hotel. I folded my arms across my chest to flatten any suspicious bulges.

"Didn't you read the signs? No Pedestrians includes bicycles."

I turned on the respect, but not too heavy. "No, sir, I must have missed them."

He was still seated too low and comfortably for me to go into full panic mode. He did some police work. "Where do you live?"

"Amherst."

"Massachusetts?"

"Yes, sir."

"What are you doing here?"

"I'm on vacation," I said, careful not to sound flip.

"And you're what, just out sightseeing?" I nodded. "On that bike?"

"Yes, sir."

"Where were you planning on going?"

"I thought I might make it to the bridge."

"That bridge?"

I nodded.

"Well, that's not going to happen." He grew six inches. "Where are you staying?"

"At my sister's in East Falmouth. Opal Cove Road."

"And you took Twenty-eight? The whole way?"

I nodded again. He sighed and opened his door without warning. He got out of the cruiser. Turns out he wasn't much taller than me.

"I really didn't know it was illegal," I said.

"You haven't been drinking, have you?"

"No."

"Because it's not warm out, and you're sweating pretty good."

"It's a hard bike to ride. And I'm out of shape."

He looked at the bike and then at me. Both things I said made sense to him. He walked to the rear of the cruiser, opened the trunk, and started shifting things. "There's a Dunkin' Donuts just up the road. I'm going to

Joe Pernice

drop you off, and you're going to figure out the rest from there."

"Okay."

"I don't care how you get yourself back to East Falmouth. But what you're not going to do is bike or walk or roller-skate or anything on Route Twenty-eight. Understood?"

"Understood."

"Because if I let you go, and you get picked up by someone else further up the road . . . you don't want that."

"I won't."

"Or if, God forbid, I pick you up again . . ."

"You won't."

"Good." It took two normal tries, then a more serious one to close the Crown Vic's trunk. "You're going to have to sit in back. All my radar's up front." I got in the cage. The sound of him auto-locking the doors had an opposite effect on my sense of security. "Seat belt on," he said.

As we were merging back onto 28, another cruiser pulled up and blocked our path. This cop was older. He looked like Boris Yeltsin. A large chief's badge was painted in gold on his door.

"What he do?" asked Captain Kickass.

"Just biking in the wrong place. He didn't know."

"Biking?"

"That's what I said to him." They shared a quick laugh about it.

"He's not Colombian, is he?"

My cop looked back at me, wordlessly passing along the question.

"Irish," I said. "American Irish."

"He's Irish."

"I'm looking for a Colombian—about his age—who likes to beat up on his pregnant wife. Knocked her to the floor and kicked her across the room."

"Scumbag."

"Real scumbag. This guy married?"

I leaned forward, right up against the cage and spoke directly to Captain Kickass. I wanted to eliminate the possibility of any miscommunication that might land me in the tank. "Separated, sir."

"Where's your wife?"

"She lives in New York."

"You ever hit her?"

"I've never hit anyone in my life."

"Nobody?"

"No, sir."

"Never been in a fistfight? Not a single time?"

"Never, sir."

He spent about a month looking through that cage, into my eyes. "Yeah, well I have." He smiled. "Plenty of times." Without lifting his foot off the brake, he shifted the cruiser into drive. It made a false start. "Let's keep the bikes on the back roads."

"I will, sir."

"And if you see any Colombians . . ." He winked and

Joe Pernice

peeled out of the dirt road. We stayed put until the rooster tail of dust settled.

The cop turned to me. "That's not really true about never hitting anyone before, is it?"

"It is."

"Wow."

THE COP HIT the Dunkin' Donuts drive-through before letting me out.

"You want anything? Guys on the force don't pay."

"No, thanks."

The drive-through girl's spiel came through the tiny speaker.

"Who's that? Brenda?" the cop asked into the menu board.

"Tommy?" she answered.

"Ten-four."

"No, it's me, Georgette."

"Chripesakes," Tommy said. "You sound more like each other every day."

"Looking like her, too," Georgette said, not too pleased about it.

"Hey, hey, enough of that," Tommy said. "You could do worse. A lot worse."

"I don't know about that," Georgette said. She yelped when an offended hand—presumably Brenda's—slapped a naked, fleshy part of her. "See what I have to put up with, Tom?"

Brenda overrode her: "You mean see what I have to put up with?"

"You could both do a lot worse," Tommy said.

"We'll see about that," Georgette said. "Large with milk and two Sweet'N Lows?"

Tommy turned to me. "You sure you don't want anything?"

"I'm sure."

"That'll do it. Large with milk and two Sweet'N Lows." He drove around to the pickup window. Georgette had his coffee waiting. Her mother stood behind her. Both women were overweight and at different points of the same free fall. They saw me in the back.

"Who's that?" the daughter asked.

Tommy reached out for the coffee. "Nobody."

"What he do?" the mother asked.

"Nothing."

"Why's he in the back?"

"Is he dangerous?"

"No, he broke down. I'm just giving him a hand."

Both women shifted their eyes to him. "That's good of you, Tom," the daughter said. "You guys"—she shook her head in admiration of all cops—"you're always sticking your necks out for other people."

"People who don't even appreciate it," the mother added. "Boy, Tom, I tell you, I sure do."

"Me, too," the daughter said.

"That's nice to hear." He started to dig some money out of his pants pocket. "It makes this job——"

The daughter waved him off. "No, no, no, no, Tom. I couldn't charge you."

Tommy stopped himself before completely saying the word *but*. It was one of the weakest "No, let me pay" protests I'd ever seen.

"It's just a cup of coffee, Tom," the mother chimed in. "What's it, two cents to them?" She said it as if the moneygrubbing Dunkin' Donuts head honchos were just out of earshot.

"Not even," the daughter added.

"You guys." Tommy stopped digging for money. He turned to me. "Can you believe these two?"

I couldn't.

"Call it one of those what-do-you-call-its," the mother said.

TOMMY LET ME off at a brown fiberglass picnic table next to the pay phone. Before he drove away, he asked me if I was sure I was feeling okay. He seemed like a decent guy for a cop.

I sat on the picnic table with my feet up on the bench. It was a beautiful day. The kind you expect it to be when you get the phone call notifying you that someone close to you has died unexpectedly. I lit a smoke, then took the wineskin out from under my coat. I took a healthy pull of Jameson's.

"What the fuck am I going to do?"

Georgette and her mother were eyeballing me through the plate glass. I turned my back to them. There was the Bourne Bridge, dizzying, spiritual, and off-limits. There'd be no epiphany on it for me today. I called James and asked him for a lift. He asked me how I ended up way the fuck up there. I told him I got lost.

IT WAS PISSING RAIN when I woke up. I was thinking about the woman who lost her shit and faked being pregnant after James cheated on her with my sister. I felt horrible. I decided to call Jocelyn's answering machine and let her know that I didn't walk out on her for someone else. I biked over to Spunt's Gas and Grocery to use the pay phone. I didn't even bother trying to stay dry.

"Can I have three of that in quarters?" I interrupted the kid behind the counter. His head was the size of a large pomegranate. He couldn't quite figure out how to make it work so that my change would include three dollars in quarters. I didn't want to embarrass him, so I just hung back and let him struggle through it.

"I have to do it all over," he said, frustrated and apologetic.

"It's okay." He gave me back my twenty, put the rest of the money in the register, and started over.

"You want gas?" he asked for the second time.

I shook my head again. I started thinking about that film clip of the Vietnam War protester who doused himself and his baby daughter with gasoline on the Pentagon lawn. The cops managed to talk the guy into letting the baby go unharmed before he torched himself. I wondered if the whisked-away baby was found by the fiery fuse that yoked her to her father.

"Eleven dollars and nine cents." The kid looked at me over his water-spotted glasses. I paid him again. The drops beating against the windows made the outside look like the inside of an aquarium.

I put my change in the plastic bag with my stuff. "Take it easy," I said, and bolted out across the flooded parking lot into a phone booth.

Automobiles hydroplaned along Plymouth Street merely a few feet away. They shrieked by like bomber jets flying to and from a common objective. I lit a smoke and snaked through the curves of my conundrum. I wanted to talk to Jocelyn, but I didn't want to talk to her. I told myself if she answered, I'd hang up. It was answering machine or nothing.

I bent down to pick up the cellophane from my cigarette pack. The corners of the phone booth floor were grouted with a cured bead of grime. It reminded me of the shitty places I'd lived, and all the shitty ones to come. Jocelyn was the cleanest person I'd ever met. I loved her towels. They were luxurious and always thirsty. She bought expensive microbrew shampoos from Sweden. She was twenty-four and she had tablecloths. She said she liked what she liked. God, I fucking envied her for knowing that.

"I'M A BIG FAN of circumcision," Jocelyn said as she washed my back with a chunk of sea sponge harvested from someplace in the Indian Ocean.

"Lucky for me." I held on to the towel bar at the back of her shower.

"It's sleeker."

Jocelyn's father was Catholic, but technically, since her mother was Jewish, so was she. I grew up Catholic. My circumcision was motivated by who knows what. Vanity or a cutthroat, lose-the-deadweight mentality. The human appendix isn't pulling its weight, either, but no one has it removed until it's practically gangrenous.

"If you ever try to convert," Jocelyn said, "a rabbi is going to have to sign off on the surgeon's work. Could have left it too long." She said it like she was talking about a haircut I could just pop in and have Lamont tidy up.

"Why would I ever convert?"

"I don't know. I'm just saying if you ever did."

"Jesus Christ, can you imagine getting recircumcised at my age?"

"People do it."

"Fucking barbaric."

"You'd think they'd have developed a nonsurgical method, you know, like a chemical peel or something."

I saw an opportunity. I reached back and pulled her arms around me. I assumed the position like I was about to be frisked by a cop. She started soaping me up. Our minds headed down the same path but quickly veered in different directions.

"You know what?" she asked.

"Mmm."

"The word *blowjob* is a total misnomer."

"Huh?"

"Think about it. There isn't a lot of blowing going on. That can be confusing when you're just starting out." She drifted as she continued working me up into a good lather. "He was almost six years older than me, so I was nervous enough as it was, you know?"

"Who?"

"Todd."

"Right," I said. "Todd."

Todd was a numskull pizza jockey and Jocelyn's first real boyfriend. She started working—as a toppings prep—and became sexually active when she was fourteen. When I was fourteen, I was still bumming occasional Pop Rocks money off my parents and dreaming of whisking Victoria Principal away with me on my personal spacecraft.

"I could feel him getting softer, so I kept blowing faster and faster. I didn't know." She huffed like she was in childbirth. "Then he pulled me really hard by the hair."

Jocelyn loosely grabbed a handful of my hair like my head was a bunch of carrots. "And I could feel him get hard again." She tightened her grip.

"That really hurts."

JOCELYN WAS a three-ringer, tops. If she didn't pick before the fourth ring, she was either not picking up or not home. Her answering machine was set to kick in two rings after that.

I went over my script as my index finger swung like a divining rod drawn to the Brooklyn area code. I felt something like a serial dieter who flirts with failure by nibbling on the first frosting rose. I dialed the rest of her number. The receiver felt cold and oily against my ear. A recording dared me to deposit an additional $1.75 for the first three minutes. I choked the coin slot with quarters.

During the first three rings I was scared she'd pick up. After the fourth I was relieved. After the fifth, sixth, seventh, eighth, ninth, and tenth rings I was wondering what the fuck was going on. Probably dialed the wrong number. I did it all again more carefully. Same thing.

"What the fuck?" No answering machine was a new development. I went over the possible explanations: (1) The machine had—after fuck knows how many years of functioning perfectly—finally broken down. (2a) The machine had become disconnected by accident. (2b) The machine had become disconnected on purpose.

I watched the last of the rain ooze down the length of the phone booth. With zero hesitation, I dialed Jocelyn's work number. There was no answer at her extension. I was rerouted to the receptionist. I told her I was an old friend. She said Jocelyn was—if I could believe it—on her honeymoon.

"Really? Do you have any idea where she went?"

"Somewhere warm. Other than that, she wouldn't say."

"You talked to her?"

"Just this morning. *Très* mysterious. *Très romantique.*"

"How did she sound?"

"How did she sound? She just got married, for goodness' sake."

I CALLED JOCELYN'S apartment again. This time I wanted her to answer. Nothing. I went back into Spunt's and bought a postcard of the Bourne Bridge.

"We only have the other kind of stamps," the kid said.

"Fine."

"And you have to buy a book of them."

"Whatever." I took a pen from beside the register and went back to the counter where the coffeepots were. I addressed the postcard to Jocelyn. I chose the rest of my words carefully: "There's no one else, by the way." I dropped the postcard in the first mailbox I saw.

I regretted it immediately because I felt like I was giving her the upper hand by being the first to crack. I mean, I knew that even if Jocelyn was under someone else, there was no way she was already over me.

RICHIE ANSWERED THE PHONE. He put his hand over the mouthpiece and mouthed, "Jocelyn again." It was the third call in less than an hour. "No," he said to her. "He's still not back yet." He listened. "I've got it written down right here." He tapped a notepad on the kitchen table with the point of a pen. "As soon as he gets in. You got it." He hung up and sighed, "Dude, not good, dude."

"Fuck me." I threw my head back and stared at the ceiling.

Richie got up and headed to the fridge. He liked being on the sidelines of other people's dramas. It gave him a chance to offer a sympathetic beer. "Why don't you just tell her you don't want to break up for good, but you need some space to figure shit out?"

"I did," I said, exasperated.

"And?"

I pointed to the phone. "She's not fucking giving me space, obviously."

"Well, fuck it. If she won't give it to you, take it." He traced the phone cord back to the wall and disconnected it from the jack. "Until further notice, this phone only makes outgoing calls." To him it was that simple.

"I can't do that to her."

"Why? You're already screening your calls, so what the fuck's the difference?" He was right. Just what I needed: more contradiction, guilt, and confusion. Richie wagged the end of the cord. "It's no skin off my ass. I hate the telephone anyway."

I buried my face in my hands. "Fuck," I yelled. Kev or Bri in the downstairs apartment turned their stereo down. "I feel like a fucking asshole."

"Why?"

"Because she's a good person. She's a great person. If she wasn't so intense . . ."

"No one's saying she isn't a good person. But you're a good person, too."

"I feel like a bleached shit."

"You shouldn't. Look, you guys had some amazing times, but the thing's fatally flawed. Whose fault is that? Nobody's fault."

His words bounced right off me. "You know what's really fucked up? I'm doing the exact shit she predicted I'd do all along."

"How do you mean?"

"Correction, not everything she predicted. I never cheated on her. Honest to God, I'd tell you if I did. But as far as me abandoning her—"

Richie cut me off. "Abandon?" he asked incredulously. "Abandon's what you do to babies and three-legged dogs."

IT WAS ALMOST nine at night when I woke up. I was starving. I biked down to the Crow's Nest. The autumn night air was seasoned with smoke from wood-burning stoves. It reminded me of playing street hockey as a kid with my friends. The bald tennis ball would grow more invisible as the evening wore on. We'd play until our mothers were nearly irate from unsuccessfully calling us to dinner. I loved it.

The restaurant was dead. They ran a dinner special anyway, perhaps out of pride. I stood just inside the doorway and read the board. Baked haddock, rice pilaf, and a cup of corn chowder. Seven ninety-five. As a rule, I steer clear of all meal specials. Once you work in a restaurant, you order differently. At Esposito's, Lello ran specials when the outermost veal cutlet in the package was freezer-burned just beyond use.

The cook got up from a table when he saw I was staying for dinner. He took his coffee and smoke with him into the kitchen. He let out a series of increasingly productive coughs. My waiter was a little red fire hydrant. His forearms were smudged with illegible tattoos. He called me Captain.

I watched the cook preparing my chicken Parmesan over egg noodles through the food pickup window. I was hoping to catch him picking his nose or his teeth. At least that way I'd be sure.

A large oval dish nested in an insulating cloth napkin slid from the waiter's hands onto my table like a foal from its mother's birth canal.

"Makes me think I'll never feel hungry again," I said. He was no audience whatsoever. I poked at the food like I was examining a pet's stool for an ingested coin. I had two beers with my meal, and nursed a healthy Jameson's on the rocks afterward. I wasn't eager to go back to the empty house.

"Anything else before we close up, Captain?" He slid the bill under my drink coaster and waited for me to pay up.

"Would it be okay if I just sat here for a little bit?" I showed him the remainder of my cocktail.

"For a little bit, sure."

He went back by the register. I lit a smoke. Todd Rundgren came over the stereo, singing, "Hello It's Me." It fucking figured. I used to like Todd Rundgren a lot until he got contaminated. I started going out with Jennifer, my first serious girlfriend, in the fall of our senior year of high school. After we made out for the first time, she iced me down by saying she was years away from having sex. I told her I was willing to wait. Months later, on the fourteenth fairway of the Presidents

Golf Course in Quincy, I managed to finger her through a tear in her jeans that was all the way down at her knee. I tried—with little success—to get into her pants via the conventional routes. And then I college-tried.

A couple of weekends later Jennifer visited her brother at the University of New Hampshire. I didn't want her to go, but she said September was less than three months away. It was important that she get used to being at UNH. Plus, it was Spring Fling Weekend, and she'd always wanted to see Terence Trent D'Arby. I told her I would have skipped seeing *London Calling*–era Clash to be with her as much as possible. She said she'd never ask me to do something like that. It made me feel like shit. When she didn't call me until the day after she got back home, I feared fall was coming a season early.

We were in the Bickford's House of Pancakes in Brockton when she told me "something happened" between her and her brother's roommate. She wouldn't go into detail. She said it didn't matter anyway because it had nothing to do with her not wanting to go out with me anymore. She was young. She wanted to date all kinds of people. I was crushed. I asked her to marry me. She tried breaking my fall by saying she wished we'd met when we were twenty-seven instead of seventeen. I would have forfeited the entire meddling decade.

She handed me a cassette she'd made especially for the occasion. It had one song on it: "Can We Still Be Friends" by Todd Rundgren. She said it summed up exactly what she wanted to say. I said there was no way we could still be friends. She thought that was too bad, but if that's how I felt, there was nothing she could do about it.

It was after eleven p.m. Her brother, his girlfriend, and his roommate appeared in the Bickford's foyer. The waitress tried to seat them, but they said they weren't staying. Jennifer got up. She told me to please listen to the tape. She joined the other three. The roommate was a UNH crew Nazi. I'd never met the guy, but he wanted to kick my ass. He was still sneering at me as Jennifer and her brother led him out the door.

I listened to the Rundgren tune a bunch of times, parked in my parents' driveway. I tried to read deep into the lyrics and twist their meaning so they'd support my hope of hopes that Jennifer would beg me to take her back. But what I heard was what I got. As far as Jennifer was concerned, I was the past. That night I cried myself to sleep. I woke up the next morning to my old man tapping on the driver's-side window.

From then on, all of Todd Rundgren's music was off-limits. That included bands he produced, such as the Psychedelic Furs and XTC. It was a shame, really. None of it was Todd Rundgren's fault. It was almost time to start thinking about thinking about forgiving him.

I SAT ON Sweet Thunder in the Crow's Nest lot and had a smoke. The stars looked like a spray of luminescent grapeshot. A station wagon full of rowdy high school kids pulled in from Plymouth Street. The car was covered in green and gold streamers and bar soap graffiti. The Sister Sledge tune "We Are Family" was punishing the speakers' tiny woofers. The driver tried three times to do a doughnut. I moved well out his way.

A girl yelled out the window, "Nice bike, queer bait." The car accelerated with youthful aggression onto Plymouth Street and disappeared into the darkness. If they all got killed it wouldn't be because I wished it on them.

I biked along the beach. Two holdout fishermen were surf-casting from within the glow of a trash can of fire. The lures dangling from their rods were as big as a fish I'd have been proud to catch. I left the bike where it fell and walked toward the light like a dead man not quite sure if he's ready for the afterlife. Regular people were home sleeping or watching the news. I coughed loudly as I got closer. The crashing waves made the beach sound like an airport.

I finally yelled, "Any luck yet?" like I was about to traipse through a grizzly bear's pantry. The colossus in the rubber hip waders and New England Patriots parka locked in on me. He gestured no a single time, then went back to fishing, like I wasn't even there. The other fisherman did absolutely nothing to acknowledge me. He, too, might have been a lure set up to tempt a big one right onto the shore.

By my third and last cigarette, it became apparent that neither man nor mannequin was going to have any good luck. And I wish I had split on that note. But I stuck around just long enough to identify in me a kinship with these fisherman ghosts.

I started thinking about the bellboy who'd carried Jocelyn's backpack into our honeymoon suite. He looked younger than me. I tipped him five bucks. He said he and his retirement savings thanked me. There wasn't a single cunt hair of sarcasm in his voice.

I WOKE UP in my shoes and clothes. The morning sky was the color of a gray polyester shirt. I got up and kept the moving blanket thrown over my shoulders like I was Crazy Horse. Certifiably Crazy Horse.

James had had the environmentally unsound idea of turning a well-used kerosene lamp into a bird feeder. I stood at the kitchen sink window and polished off a box of toffee popcorn. I took a drink from the faucet. The water was so cold it hurt one of my molars. I hadn't seen a dentist in years because I was afraid of what he'd have to do to fix me. I dug my knuckle hard into my jawbone to crimp the furious nerve.

The next-door neighbor's woodpile taunted me from an open-faced shed painted to match the house. The only fireplace in my sister's was boarded up. I considered pinching some wood and building a campfire in the back-yard, but I knew James would blow a gasket.

I started thinking about an episode of *The Beverly Hill-billies* where Granny sets a fire—complete with kindling and logs——in the electric oven. It should have been funny, but it just made me sad. Like when I was in fifth grade, and me and a few other students were tapped to demonstrate to the new first-graders the proper way to use a urinal. When Sister Catherine John asked if I'd be willing to help them out, I felt very grown up. Seconds after I agreed, I wished I hadn't. Before I could show him the right way to do it, little Timmy Homesick dropped his drawers, sat on the urinal, and took a shit in it.

That bird feeder worried me.

JOCELYN AND I were bored stiff, so we rode the ferry to Staten Island and back. That night she took me to a gourmet Peruvian restaurant in the Village that seats ten people. The food was pretty good, but way the fuck out there, and the portions were too small. I leaned across the table and whispered something about feeling guilty for eating some poor kid's iguana. Usually a good line like that would have caused her to laugh her balls off.

The cab ride back to her place was a pretty quiet one. I put my hand on her thigh. She smiled, but stopped me from doing any impromptu spelunking. When we got home, we watched *Cries and Whispers* in bed as planned. Afterward she gave me an unsolicited, low-passion hand job. Then I asked her what she wanted me to do to her. She told me to let her go to sleep. I asked her if she still loved me, and she said yes. I had to work the dinner shift on Sunday, so I caught an early bus back to Amherst. Connecticut always was—and always will be—the state in my way. Somewhere between the pilonidal cyst that is Stamford and the perforated bowel that is New Haven, I felt something with my foot under the seat in front of me. I drew it closer. It was a royal blue three-ringed binder. It said Bank of New York in white. It belonged to one Viola Sporney. I flipped through it. It was full of pink Bank of New York forms executed by Viola. I couldn't make any sense of them. The last page was white. On it was a hand-written to-do list:

1. Monday: Research D and MacC props. Get OK from O'Banyon.

2. Tuesday: Check financials for L.D. Get OK from O'Banyon.

3. Wednesday: Start Jogging.

I phoned Jocelyn when I got home and read her the to-do list. No, she didn't think it was that depressing.

I WENT TO SEE a shrink once at UMass. He said me being on Prozac was the right move. As soon as I heard that, I turned him off for three reasons: (1) I didn't want to risk anyone finding out. (2) You'd practically have to throttle your dick to death before you could come (a non-issue). (3) Prozac made Del Shannon kill himself.

I backpedaled and told the shrink that maybe I'd exaggerated some of my story, and that just talking about it had me feeling better. A lot better. He didn't buy it, but what was he going to do, force-feed me antidepressants? It wasn't like I was opening veins or making bombs in my dorm room.

I finished the semester, landing squarely on academic probation. I went home to my childhood twin bed in suburban Boston. I got my old summer job back, packing orders in an office-supply warehouse in East Bridgewater. Del Shannon's tormented voiced lifted my spirits during rush-hour traffic jams on Route 24. I had always thought of Del Shannon as being right down there with Pat Boone. Why? Because I didn't know what the fuck I was talking about. The part where Del wonders where she will stay, his little runaway? And the chorus of "I Go to Pieces"? Fuck me. They're still hard to listen to.

The small-headed kid at Spunt's pointed at me from behind the counter. "Hey, look, it's Pay Phone." It was better than being called Dogshit.

"Hey." I grabbed a special three-for-the-price-of-two pack of Winstons. I speed-read the J-cards of the cassette tapes that filled a lazy Susan. There was no Del Shannon.

"You don't need a job, do you?" the kid asked. He was twirling a point-of-purchase pinwheel sticking out of a bouquet of them.

"No, but thanks, anyway."

"I do. If I didn't have a job, I'd be nobody."

When I got back to the house, James was waiting there to pass Roy off on me. He already had him strapped into the stroller.

"I didn't think you were going to show," James said.

"That's funny, because I knew you would."

"IT'S SAD WHEN anyone dies, Roy." I pushed the stroller along our usual route. One of the small, bone-jarring wheels was seized up. "Even bad people." Opal Cove Road was a dead-end street. Number 97 was the last house on the left. It was a weather-beaten ranch identical to my sister's. It didn't appear to be in worse shape than any of the other houses left unattended for seven of the year's harshest months. All of the window shades were drawn. The front lawn was sand and twigs. There was a wet case of empty Bud Light cans at the end of the driveway. I looked around, then scooped it up. I jammed the case into the stroller's mesh undercompartment. I had never returned cans that were not of my own—or my party's own—emptying. But twenty-four cans was a buck twenty. Smokes were two-fifty a pack. I'd come a long way, baby.

A few days later, when I took care of Roy again, there was another case of empties and a beat-up Subaru wagon in the driveway of 97 Opal Cove Road.

"Let's get the fuck out of here, kid."

I heard the unmistakable sound of a dog's collar jangling at charging speed. A muscular Doberman rounded the corner of the house and stopped at a safe sizing-up distance. He growled like a wood chipper. Raw egg white saliva swung from his fangs. I moved slightly, and so did he. Roy and I were pinned.

"Go home!" I ordered. "Go home!" The dog did not obey.

"Tinker, no!" someone screamed. "Tinker, no!"

I located the source of the voice. Marie was standing on the back porch of 97 Opal Cove Road. She started banging a large metal watering jug with a gardening shovel. "Is this your fucking dog?" I yelled.

"No, Tinker! No, Tinker!"

Roy started to freak. He tried desperately to squirm his restrained body higher up the stroller's seat. The Doberman lunged at his feet and clamped onto his pant leg. I wrested Roy free. Tinker pulled back empty-mouthed. He was not fucking around. If I didn't do something, he was going to eat Roy.

"Tinker!" Marie screamed.

"It's okay, Roy," I lied. "Go home!" I screamed at Tinker. I lifted Roy—stroller and all—onto the hood of the Subaru.

Tinker attacked me before I could follow Roy to relative safety. The savage was locked onto my left desert boot at the Achilles tendon. He started whipping his head back and forth like a well-hooked tarpon. I sledgehammered my fist wildly at his mouth. I was pounding the piss out of my own foot in the process. Tinker was trying to snap my ankle's neck. I didn't feel any of it. Roy was screaming.

"Off, Tinker!" Marie ordered. I heard a series of low-pitched, hollow *gonk*s as she beat the dog's upholstered rib cage with the watering can. She brought it down so hard on his head my boot came off. Tinker yelped and retreated through the hedges that separated two yards.

"He has my fucking shoe." I was shaking.

"The baby!" Marie screamed. Roy was facing us, crying as the stroller rolled backward in slow motion toward the edge of the hood. I grabbed the exposed calf of his fat drumstick. Marie took hold of the stroller and lowered it to the driveway. Roy screamed louder.

"Oh, God, no," she said. "He's hurt." She raised his pant leg. His skin was a bloody mess.

"Oh-fuck-oh-fuck-oh-fuck-oh-fuck-oh-fuck. Fuck me, Roy! Oh, fuck, no!"

"Calm down!" Marie took off her sweatshirt and used it to dab his leg. She was wearing a white tanktop. She had a detail from the *Apocalpyse Now* movie poster tattooed on her biceps.

I was close to crying. "He's just a baby. He's just a fucking baby."

"It's okay," she said. "It's okay. I think it's your blood."

My hands were covered in it. I looked away. I saw my desert boot lying like a mountaineering accident at the edge of the driveway. "Are you sure?"

"I'm pretty sure."

．　．　．

I WAS AWAKENED in the early hours of the morning by the sound of someone tapping their keys on the pressed-steel storm door.

"Who the fuck?" I said, like my old man trying to eat a single hot supper in peace. I got up and slid on my pants. The tight, quiet ache in my punctured heel spiked and burned as my foot passed through my pant leg. The tapping on the door grew more desperate. I flipped the porch light on and opened the door.

Marie was standing there with no coat on. I knew drunk when I saw it.

"Please help me," she slurred.

"Are you hurt?"

She dismissed me. "No, no, no. I just need sleep." She reminded me of Judy Garland leaning into Steve Allen—or whoever the fuck it was—on TV. She tried to push me aside and enter the house. I held firm.

"No, no, no, no, no, come on. Don't do that."

"Just right there." She pointed to the living room floor behind me. She crouched below my tollbooth arm and attempted to squeeze between me and the doorframe. I pinched her off.

"I'm sorry. You can't."

She raised her face close to mine. Her breath was a vodka aerosol. "I saved your baby."

"I know, and I appreciate it. But you have to go home."

"But I saved it. The baby. Let me see him." She tried to get by me again.

"He's not here."

"Where is he?"

"At his mother's."

"Then let's go get him."

"We can't get him."

"Why not?" She wasn't the worst kind of drunk, but a bad-enough one: she wanted to be reasoned with.

"He's a baby. He's asleep."

"Fuck you, then. Thanks." She said something I couldn't understand. Her upper and lower halves raced each other back to her car, which was still running and nearly perpendicular to the sidewalk. She had only a few hundred yards to drive, and it was so early in the morning, the only person she could hurt was herself.

"Fuck it," she hollered, then threw up on the hood.

I watched her for a few seconds trying to mop the hood of the car with her sleeve. "Fuck it," I said. I grabbed a T-shirt and went after her.

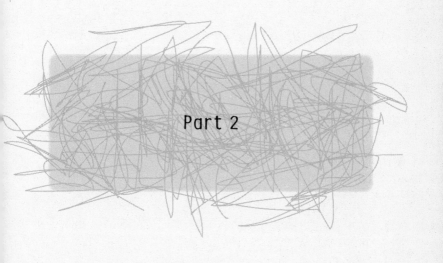

Part 2

I HAD A one-nighter in college that turned into a one-weekender. Another friend-of-a-friend thing. Her name was Julie. On Sunday afternoon I could tell Julie was getting too attached. She kept saying—in a blushing, pleasantly surprised way—that she never did things like this. She also thought it was cute the way I had to sleep with socks on. So I made sure my Friday-night disclaimer was still fresh in her mind. She had just bounded in from the kitchen, back to her futon with a tuna salad sandwich on toasted seven-grain bread. She took *Court and Spark* out of the tape player. She said she understood that I was unavailable for anything more, but that she couldn't say she wasn't disappointed. She thought maybe the weekend had changed my mind. I told her I didn't think it had. I felt shitty about the whole thing. I didn't want to sleep over her place that night, but I did anyway.

I woke up in Marie's bed. She was getting dressed in the early-morning gray. She parted the curtains. The room went Technicolor. I faked the tail end of sleep and watched her. She was about the same height as Jocelyn, but thicker in almost every way. She picked up some clothes off the floor like she was cleaning up a careless mistake. A tattoo snake rose up the back of her neck and buried its head in her short black bob.

My head was spinning and I was thirsty. I thought about what I was going to say to her. I finally sat up and lit a smoke. Marie kept looking the other way.

"Hey," I said.

"Hey."

"How you feeling?"

"Like shit."

"I'm not great, but I'll live."

She stayed as far away from me as she could without leaving the room. She lit a smoke from the pack on her dresser and finally faced me. Her eyes were saddled and dark. "How exactly did you get here?"

I told her.

She nodded. "Did I suck you off?"

"You tried to, but—"

"But you stopped me."

I nodded.

"Did we fuck?"

"No." I peeled back the covers to show I was still wearing my pants. "We made out, but nothing really happened."

"I'm sorry."

She was sorry? I wasn't expecting an apology. "Don't be, please. Nothing happened." I got up and started to gather the rest of my clothes.

"It's not fucking you I'm sorry about."

"But we didn't."

"I don't care if we did. I'm sorry for showing up at your door in the middle of the night wasted."

"You weren't that wasted," I lied.

"When you can't remember if you let a perfect stranger come in your mouth . . ." She was leaning against a desk. She put her head down. "I'm just sorry, that's all."

"Okay." If that had been Jocelyn there on the other side of the room, I don't know what she would have done to me. She sure as fuck wouldn't have apologized.

"ROY'S GETTING really big," I said.

Pamela grunted as she extracted him from the car seat. "Tell me about it." She looked tired but, on the whole, the best I'd seen since before she'd had Roy. Maybe it was the clothes. She wasn't wearing one of her usual frumpy Sears pantsuits.

I touched her turtleneck sweater. "Is that cashmere?"

"Silk," she said proudly.

"Nice."

"I figured, what the hell, right?"

Roy's feet hit the sidewalk, and he ran directly into my arms. "Hey, buddy, remember me?"

Pamela lit up. "Wow. He only goes to people he really knows."

"That is so amazing."

"It's only because you and I have the same nose."

"No, it's more than that."

"You think?"

"You're a natural. I told you so."

"Natural what?" Roy tried to reprise the glasses-swiping game.

"Gentle, baby," Pamela said. "Gen-tull."

"It's okay." I folded my glasses and put them in my pocket. Roy was pissed off. He hollered.

"It's okay, baby." Pamela distracted him with the small flashlight on her key chain. "He's at that age where he wants everything. And if you don't give it to him, watch out."

No shit.

"He bit my neck the other day, look." She rolled back the foreskin of her turtleneck. There was a purple bruise over her carotid artery.

"Holy shit. He got you pretty good. What did you do to get that?"

"I wouldn't let him have a lightbulb."

"Oh, Christ."

"I know, right?"

"Sounds rough."

"It *is* rough. Really rough. But it's easier, too, in some ways, if you know what I'm talking about." She didn't want to say too much in front of Roy. "Has he been around much?"

"Who? James?"

"No," she said with the kind of sarcasm that has sunk many a sitcom pilot. "Yes, James."

"A couple times, quick. Him and Dogshit." Pamela shook her head at the mention of his name. "They stopped by and fixed something. Fuck if I know what."

"Easy with the language," Pamela said. "He's starting to repeat things."

"Sorry." I turned to Roy. "Sorry, kid. Don't do what I do."

"You sound just like Dad," Pamela said. Countless times I've heard my father say those very words—don't do what I do—seconds before doing something like stick a screwdriver into a dark recess of a running car engine. "Him and Ma been down yet?" She sounded like she was privy to something I wasn't.

"You fucking told them I'm here?"

"No, I did not. And watch your mouth, please." Roy

recognized the annoyed and imperative qualities in his mother's voice. He stopped jiggling the keys and gave us his undivided attention. Pamela softened. "But you know how they are. Empty house. Neighbors gone for the winter. I wouldn't be surprised if they drive down once a week to make sure nobody stole the paint off the shutters."

She was right. "Or the sconces," I added.

"Or the sconces."

Our parents were mildly insane that way. It should have been much funnier than it was. Roy was smiling.

"What about 'Show me the couch'?" I said. It was a famous story in our family.

"Oh, Christ almighty." Now it was Pamela who sounded like our father.

When Pamela was sixteen, she volunteered to hang out at our aunt Christie's apartment in East Boston and sign for the new couch that Jordan's Furniture was delivering sometime between nine in the morning and four in the afternoon. My aunt Christie was an air-traffic controller at Logan Airport and couldn't miss work. Her apartment was on the top floor of a four-story walk-up.

My old man was not into the idea of Pamela's being alone with three or four furniture movers, as it's well documented how fond furniture movers are of squeezing unscheduled gang rapes into their busy days.

My old man walked Pamela through the correct answers, then quizzed her:

Old Man: And what are you going to say when the movers buzz up from the lobby?

Pamela: Who is it?

OM: And when they knock on Aunt Christie's door, then what are you going to say?

P: Who is it?

OM: And after they identify themselves as the movers, and you see them through the peephole, what are you going to say before letting them in?

P: Just a minute, I'm naked?

OM: Don't be a smart-ass. I'm serious here.

P: Show me the couch. I say, "Show me the couch."

OM: Exactly. Show me the couch.

I took a smoke from my pack, and Pamela motioned wordlessly, like a blackjack player who wants the dealer to keep 'em comin'.

"You don't smoke," I said.

"Oh, shut up." She tickled Roy's chin and said in a cartoon voice, "Show me the couch. Your grandparents are crazy, crazy, crazy." He collapsed in a giggling heap on the driveway. Pamela turned to me. "But you are going to have to tell them you guys split up, you know?"

"Thanks," I said sarcastically. "I had no fucking idea."

"I'm just saying, you might want to do it sooner than later."

"What for?"

"They're reserving the function room at the Knights of Columbus for a party for you guys."

"Are you fucking serious?"

She nodded. "Around Christmas."

"Shit."

"I told Ma you guys meant it, you didn't want a party or anything."

"What did she say?"

"That it wasn't about what you wanted."

"Fucking Ma. I swear to God, we should have kept getting married a secret."

Pamela couldn't resist. "What were you going to do, never tell anyone?"

"Not never. When we knew it was going to work out, then . . ."

"You're kidding?"

"What, is that so wrong?"

"Whatever. It's your business." She didn't want to get sucked deeper into the conversation she'd started. She took refuge in her pocketbook, feeling around in it like doing so was her sole purpose in life. "Tell me I did not forget my Visine, Roy."

"Not telling anyone certainly would have made splitting up a lot easier," I said.

Pamela responded by not responding.

I had at her. "And do me a favor. Spare me the 'You can't leave yourself a trapdoor and expect your relationship to work' crap."

"Fine. Do I look like I'm not sparing you?" She had the contents of the bag emptied onto the sidewalk.

"But you do think that, though, don't you? That you can't have a trapdoor?"

"Are you asking me or are you not asking me?"

"Yes, I'm asking you."

"The answer is no. You can't."

"Oh, okay. So you honestly thought you were going to stay married to James? Forever?"

"I didn't think it was going to be easy, but I thought I was signing on for good."

"Yeah, well, it looks like I was right, and you were wrong." That hurt her.

"Why are you being such a fucking asshole? Just because you're screwed up and having a shit time doesn't mean you get to be cruel." She was right, and I was sorry I'd hit her that hard. "And to me of all people. You call me out of the blue—"

"I know. I know. I didn't mean that." I was trying to head her off before she could recap her generosity and my selfishness. But she wasn't going to stop until she'd gone through at least one cycle of letting me know how she felt about the whole thing. I got out of her way.

"And you tell me all this crazy, über-dramatic shit—like my plate isn't buried already. You need a place to stay, a few dollars, and I say, 'No problem.'"

I felt like a shit for making her cry right in front of Roy. "You're right. I'm sorry. Please, stop crying." I touched her arm, partly so Roy would sense that affection still existed in the world. "Mommy doesn't feel so good, Roy."

Pamela regrouped.

I looked her right in the eyes. "I appreciate everything. I really do. If it wasn't for you, I'd be screwed royally."

"No you wouldn't, you idiot. You'd be inconvenienced. Confused. Scared, God forbid. And then you'd have to figure it out like every other slob. Jesus Christ."

I was going to say something smart-assed to Roy, like how Mommy was obviously feeling a lot better, but I didn't. I watched as my sister threw the former contents, one item at a time, back into the bag. When I finally spoke, it was just above a whisper. "Well, I do mean it. Thanks for helping me."

"Right." She didn't look at me as she snapped her bag closed.

"What, you want me to get out of the house?"

"No. Come on, Roy. Mommy's got to make a detour to CVS."

"Well, maybe I could watch him here and there. You know, to earn my keep."

Pamela laughed.

I WOKE UP a few hours after Jocelyn split for work. Waking up alone was one of my favorite things about New York. I had a smoke in bed and listened to the wilderness. Sixth Avenue just below Ninth Street in Brooklyn was lined with old elm and oak trees. From late spring to early fall, Jocelyn's bedroom looked out into the jiggling bosom of an enormous green sequined dress.

I was planning on going out to Shea Stadium for an afternoon guided tour. Jocelyn thought baseball was sexist, and on top of that, she wondered, why should baseball players make so much more money than teachers or social workers. I told her it was about supply and demand. She said two-thirds of the earth was covered with assholes.

Luckily for me, *Redbook* was "in ship" that week. Even Jocelyn's lunches were working ones. She was bummed out because she wanted to squeeze every last drop of together time from my visit.

Jocelyn had one of those Bodum plunger coffeemakers. They make horrible-tasting coffee. Jocelyn disagreed, which is why she had one in the first place. I called it a Scrodum instead of a Bodum. She didn't think that was too funny.

I poured the rest of the cold coffee into a three-pound mug Jocelyn received as a gift when she was a second-semester lesbian in college. The potter's name was Sue, but she went by Brianna. She and Jocelyn had a brief thing. Jocelyn was stingy when it came to divulging the details of it. I asked her if Brianna was good looking. Jocelyn said it wasn't about that. I asked her what they did in bed. She said they pretty much just made out, and, no, asshole, the first time wasn't after a Sweet Honey in the Rock concert.

I couldn't believe they didn't go any further than

making out. When I pressed her, she asked me why I wanted to know so much. I told her it was the responsible thing, what with AIDS and all. Jocelyn held up her pussy finger and wiggled it ever so slightly, then left it in the "Fuck you" position.

I brought up Sue/Brianna's names once while Jocelyn and I were fucking. It was a big no-no. She was unpredictable like that. She'd ask me to slap her on the ass now and then, but if I initiated it, she acted like I'd asked to watch the gutter bum of my choice take a piss in her mouth.

I was craving some toast, but Jocelyn only had rye bread. I didn't have any because it tastes like medicine to me. I lit another smoke and sat at the table with my coffee. My hands were shaky. The latest issue of *The New Yorker* topped a neat pile of back issues. I read a few cartoons, then got the show on the road. I took my smoke and coffee with me to the can. Jocelyn left a note for me on the back of the toilet because she knew I'd find it there: "Tried to wake you. Free for lunch, after all. Come by office. Noon sharp. xoxoj."

Fuck me. I lifted the seat cover, and the note slipped out of sight behind the shitter. Problem solved. I sat on the hoop and pulled a random issue of *Redbook* from the wicker magazine box. Cybill Shepherd was on the cover wearing a Calvin Klein tan herringbone tweed skirt and blazer ($1,995; Saks Fifth Avenue); white pinpoint Oxford shirt by Pink ($295; Pink, NYC); green armadillo cowboy boots by Justin ($895; Barneys New York).

According to the blurb on the cover, Cybill was revealing to *Redbook*'s readers her secret to having it all: children, romance, and career. I found Jocelyn's name under the junior editors' section of the masthead. Then I went straight to the Cybill Shepherd article. I jerked off to a photo spread of her—in full equestrian gear—grooming a horse named Lemonade.

Around one o'clock I called Jocelyn from Shea Stadium. I knew she'd be too busy to pitch a proper fit. I got the short form.

"Where the fuck were you?"

I could hear telephones and fax machines exploding in the background. "What are you talking about?"

"Didn't you see my note?"

"What note?"

"You know what? I can't talk to you about this now."

"What note?"

I TOSSED AND TURNED most of the night. My dog bite itched, and I was trying to calculate the size of the wrench I'd tossed into things by spending the night with Marie. It was plenty big enough to beat myself up with. I finally knocked myself unconscious. I couldn't have been asleep too long when James barged in with Roy. They were an hour early. I had no intention of telling him about Marie or the dog attack. Roy couldn't rat me out even if he wanted to.

"It's Roto-Rooter," James said. "We're here about your clog."

"Fuck, James. You said you'd be here at nine." I was not my usual ray-of-golden-sunshine self.

"Definitely not."

I pushed back at him from beneath the covers. "Definitely yes."

"Definitely not the case, but we're here now, aren't we?" He underhanded Roy on top of me. "Teach 'em a lesson about punctuality, kid."

Roy squirmed his way up like a slimy newborn kangaroo trying to make it to his mother's pouch. When he got to my head, he licked my chin. It tickled. Roy laughed after I did. Why he was so happy to see me, I had no idea. It felt pretty good, but I was suspicious.

"Pamela told me she stopped by with the kid," James said. "I assume since she didn't chew my dick down to the nub that you didn't tell her anything. But then I got to thinking, What if you did, and she was just playing dumb and collecting evidence?"

"That seems kind of elaborate."

"Maybe yes. Maybe no."

"I got to tell you, I don't feel so hot about lying to her. She's down on me as it is."

"That's crazy," James said. I was letting Roy bounce on my chest. "You and Roy can't do no wrong in her eyes."

"I still don't like lying to her."

"But you did lie, right?"

"Yeah, I lied to her."

James wasn't satisfied. "What did you say, exactly?"

"I don't know. I just pretended like I hadn't seen you in a while."

"Good. Just so long as we're on the same page." He went to the bathroom to see how his hinge repair was still holding up. "It's not really lying," he yelled. "And I'm the one who's lying anyway."

I heard him open and close the door a few times.

When he came back he said, "God, this room really stinks. Did you queef?"

"Yes. Right out of my vagina."

"I'm not kidding. It smells like a sore throat in here." He took a more forensic, sour-faced whiff. "A sore throat and old butter."

For once, he was exactly right.

JOCELYN AND I had maybe five or six "officially broken-up" periods. I initiated all of them. During the first one, I promptly slept with an older waitress at Esposito's who was into kayaking and talking about being "on her moons." Her name was Leyla. I heard every third word she said. Her face was perpetually sunburned and her hair was a blown-out yellow. She was in an open marriage with a carpenter named Dylan. She called him Dill when she referred to him—which she did a lot; it was a testament to their open-marital strength. Dill was off somewhere building houses in the Pacific Northwest. We lubed ourselves up by drinking the beer he brewed. Each brown bottle had a label with a roofer's hammer and Dill's Own Lager printed on it. As I sunk into his wife, I half expected him to pop home and sink a roofing hammer into me before driving straight back to fucking Spokane.

"It's obvious you're still in love with her," Leyla said as she wrestled herself out of her Wranglers. "Look at me and Dill. We're in love with each other. Sometimes though, you need a freebie."

"Don't take this the wrong way," I said as I stuffed my socks into my shoes to expedite my exit. "But isn't a freebie when a hooker gives you a turn on the house?"

"No. It means you do it because you're free to."

Two days later I called Jocelyn and asked her if she wanted to talk. She wanted to know why. I told her I didn't want her to move to New York, that we should get married. She said she didn't think she could count on me, but to come over anyway if I was serious about talking. We sat on her bed. The first thing she asked me was if I'd been with anyone else. I lied to her because I was ashamed and I knew she'd never let me forget it. She kept asking. She said, no, really, it would be okay, honest—especially since we were split up—as long as I told her the truth about it. Amherst is a small town. She didn't want to be the only idiot who didn't know. I resisted further. She said if I was honest with her, we could start over—right then and there—swear to God—with a clean slate. She was all smiles and understanding. I thought about Keith Richards having all of his poisoned blood replaced with a supply that was fresh, promising, and bright. I came clean—sort of. I told Jocelyn that Leyla and I had protected sex—missionary position only—one time. And by "one time" I meant I'd had a single, unsatisfying—depressing, if you really must know—semi-orgasm.

Jocelyn went totally fucking ballistic. She didn't know what was worse—that I lied to her or that I "stuck my dick into that smoky old purse." She was so upset she skinned a pillow alive, rolled the case into a ball, and threw it at a glass on her dresser.

She wanted to know how I could be so fucking cruel and vulgar? I told her I was still in love with her, and that we weren't even going out at the time. That made it worse. She started crying and said she was crushed that I could turn off my feelings for her so quickly. I told her I hadn't turned off anything. She asked me why I did it if I was still so in love with her? I think Leyla might have been right, that I just needed a freebie. But I told Jocelyn I didn't know why I did it. Jocelyn wasn't happy about that answer. I told her I'd make something up if she wanted me to. She said she'd take me back if I was absolutely explicit about what Leyla and I did to each other, where we did it, who else knew about it, et cetera. It was like she'd prepared a list long beforehand because she knew I'd be unfaithful at some point, which, technically I had not been. She made me feel like I'd been cheating on her since day one with her best friend, when all I'd done was bend the truth.

She pressed me for the details. Fool me once. I gave her the answers that I'd want to hear if I was in her position. I'd never believe them, but I'd still want to hear them.

I WAS WORRIED about getting attacked by Tinker again, but more than that, I didn't want to run into Marie. I had a growing feeling that once she sobered up and thought about it, she'd come around to blaming me for the hookup. When we took our walk, Roy and I kept away from her end of Opal Cove Road. It didn't make any difference. Marie's Subaru rolled to a stop in front of us.

"I knew it, Roy."

Marie got out but stood behind the open door. She was wearing a long, dark paisley scarf tight against her head. She looked a lot better than the last time I'd seen her.

"How is he?" she asked.

I palmed Roy's head. "Pretty good."

"Hey there, Roy," she said.

He was a loyal kid. He gave her the cold shoulder. She wasn't expecting that.

"Don't take it personally. It takes him a while to warm up to people, right, kid?" I rubbed his head. He bristled. "See what I mean?" Marie smiled weakly. I watched her watching Roy like she was waiting for him to do something remarkable. She started fidgeting with the door's foam rubber seal.

"Do you think we could get together sometime and talk?" she asked.

"Is something wrong?"

"Don't worry. It's nothing bad. Honestly."

RICHIE'S STEREO SPEAKERS were enormous. He pointed them out into the living room from his bedroom doorway. We were listening to the album *All Rise* by Naked Raygun, watching a Nuremberg trials documentary on TV with the sound off. We were stripped down to our boxers, lying on ratty, his-and-his loveseats that were too short for our bodies. The loveseats smelled like old Band-Aids. A full-on August heat wave made it seem like the living room of a forgotten elderly shut-in. At least when you're broke and it's cold, you can put on more clothes. But you can only get so naked when it's hot.

"Why in the fuck does Hitler get to own that 'stache?" Richie asked. We weren't even high, so I took it as rhetorical. He lifted his chin while pinching his upper lip. "I think I'd look good in one. But if I wore one around this town, every lefty hippie peacenik fuck would want to tear a strip off me." He was right. Amherst was one of those places that was liberal to a fault. It made you feel uncomfortable, like the person who found the unrecycled mouthwash bottle in your trash might be waiting for you in the dark.

"Melanie's beard is thicker than the one Gregory Peck grew for *Moby Dick*," Richie said, "and everyone cuts her a free pass because she's a dyke expressing herself." Melanie was a busboy at Esposito's. She was also a friend of Richie's. I brought that up. "Not the fucking point," he said. "What *is* the point is, why can't I, a decent, semi-law-abiding citizen, wear a Hitler? It's bullshit."

"Because it would bum a lot of people out."

"Why?"

"Why?" The perspiration oozing down the lovely brown hips of a Michelob bottle collected in the dent of my sternum. The ceiling was unevenly stained by secondhand smoke and seepage.

"Yeah, why? Think about it. Stalin was just as big a douche as Hitler. And he had a mustache." No arguments from me there. "Well, then why the fuck aren't mobs of people out gang-shaving Burt Reynolds or Tom Selleck?"

I egged him on. "Or what's-his-face, that dude from the Toronto Maple Leafs?"

"Wendel Fucking Clark. There's another one. Why's he still walking the streets, and I can't grow a Hitler?"

"Nobody's stopping you. Grow one."

Richie got a look on his face like it just occurred to him that buying some relatively expensive thing—a used, beater motorcycle or two work-free weeks of fucking off—were doable if he was smart about it. "Look at these fucking psychopaths," he said. A chain gang of Nazi defendants donned their translation headphones in unison. "One of the really fucked-up things is that these guys had, like, wives and shit who loved them. I mean truly loved them."

"Hard to imagine." But it wasn't really.

"This fucking guy." Richie presented a particularly horrible and homely Nazi as his case in point. "This guy's wife worshipped the ground he walked on."

"He probably persuaded her." I said it like Major Hochstetter from *Hogan's Heroes*.

"Fuck that. She always had a hot strudel waiting for him when he got home from a hard day at the Zyklon B plant."

Richie scratched at the large shamrock tattoo high on his biceps. It was a money-green reminder of a night he'd never remember. He wasn't even Irish. When I asked him why he didn't have it removed, he told me there was no point, like it was a mole his doctor told him not to worry about. I told Jocelyn the whole tattoo story, and she said Richie was a schnauxer. It was a Yiddish word she invented. A schnauxer is a guy who realizes he bought a case of the wrong shade of house paint and ends up using it anyway.

"You ever see Eichmann's old lady?" I asked.

"Nice?"

"Hell yeah. Feeders like this." I supported two enormous air tits, my beer jammed tight in their cleavage.

"You laugh. I bet you money you're not far off. And name me a bigger animal than Eichmann."

It was my turn to go to the fridge for beers. Richie did some soul-searching in the forty seconds I was gone.

"Yeah," he said, like he hated to admit it, "it's about time I got a serious girlfriend."

"Why would you do that?"

"Well, why the fuck do you have one?"

"No, I mean you hook up with more women than anyone I know. Why get tied down?"

"So, if you could trap as much pelt as me, you wouldn't be in an exclusive thing?"

"No, I would, but——"

"Damn right, you would. Your old lady's awesome. You know how fast some other dog would be sniffing her ass? They already are."

I knew Richie had a small crush on Jocelyn. I wasn't concerned. He was a good friend. In fact, I actually enjoyed knowing he liked her, because there was no way she'd ever have anything to do with him.

We stopped talking and listened to the end of the song "Peacemaker." The lead Nuremberg prosecutor was pounding sand up the ass of some kraut who had it coming.

"That guy is no bullshit," Richie said. "He never even went to college."

"No shit? How'd he get this gig?"

"You don't have to go to law school or college to take the bar exam." Richie said it like it was something he'd considered doing.

"You should take it. But wait till your Hitler's nice and full."

"That would be fucking hilarious. Distract all those Amherst College lawyer wannabes. They'd shit themselves."

"You could single-handedly change the face of the Massachusetts legal system." Richie liked that idea.

The faces of the condemned Nazis were as sullen as their victims'. One by one, black hoods turned them into footnotes before the gallows floor vanished from beneath their feet.

"Fuck it," Richie said. "I am officially growing a Hitler." He lifted the window shade to gauge if the sun was any closer to cutting us some slack. A wide blade of white sunlight momentarily obliterated the Nuremberg trials.

"I got the beers," I said. "You flip the record."

"Christ," Richie said. "It's like a fucking oven in here."

MARIE WAS PICKING me up at seven. I didn't want her to see how I was living, so I waited on the front porch. I was already at the sidewalk when she drove up.

"You have to get in this door," she said.

"I know."

"Right." She put the Subaru in park and got out. I squeezed past her. Her hair looked damp. It smelled like a banana daiquiri. I cleared the stick shifter and got myself seated. The Hefty-bag passenger window sagged in against my face.

"Sorry about the window."

"It's dark out anyway." I checked out her ass as she got back in. It looked pretty good, even in navy blue Dickies. She left the door open to keep the dome light on. She let out a sigh, like the first of many hurdles had been negotiated. Then she just sat there for what seemed like an extraordinarily long time, staring at the windshield. I pretended to think nothing of it. I looked around the car's interior like I was taking in the great room at Monticello. Marie snapped herself to attention. "Okay, let's go eat," she said, like she was psyching herself up for a Brazilian wax.

"We can do this another time if you don't feel good. I'm not even hungry."

"Please." She took my hand, and I flinched. "It's important for me to do this."

"Okay." My door had no handle. I was Ted Bundy'd in.

WE WENT TO the Crow's Nest. From across the room, the waiter and cook nodded at me when we walked in.

"Come here a lot?" Marie asked.

I didn't answer.

"Two for dinner, Captain?" the waiter asked with menus in hand.

MARIE PICKED THE chunks of meat from her lobster roll and scraped off most of the mayo before eating it. She scrubbed her front teeth with her tongue after each swallow. She looked like she was working a football mouthpiece into proper position. It was a little disgusting to watch. I deducted a few beauty points.

"So, what did you want to talk to me about?"

She took a sip of her cocktail. "Have you ever made a film?"

"No." I didn't think she was talking about porn, but I wasn't sure. Jocelyn and I had snapped a few Polaroids of each other that were bluish in tint. Garden-variety back-of-the-top-drawer stuff. But that was all. We pillow-talked about doing more, and that was arousing enough. Plus it would be a drag if my parents saw it. Or if I had a kid someday—which was never going to happen, but if I did—it would blow having sex movies of me out there.

"I'm a filmmaker." She swallowed, then pushed the sides of her hair behind her ears. "I thought maybe you'd work for me for a couple weeks." I pictured a false-walled torture chamber retrofitted to 97 Opal Cove Road. "I can't pay you a lot."

"Why me?"

"Honestly? The way you take care of that baby gave me a feeling about you."

"Really? I almost got him eaten."

"But you didn't." She took a drink. "And you didn't fuck me when I was wasted."

"If I was more shitfaced I would have."

"Thanks a lot. Am I that attractive?"

"No. Yes. I meant if I'd have had more to drink-"

She smiled. "I know what you mean. If, if, if. If I was the queen of England, I'd pee Moët."

We laughed. I felt the earliest pinch of a crush.

"Seriously," she said, "why are you trying to make me think you're repulsive for *not* being repulsive?"

"Is that what I'm doing?"

I WAS WAITING as the bus pulled into Amherst Station. It was near midnight. I'd been staring at a small cluster of fireflies flickering above a patch of unruly garbage grass, trying not to think about the family I'd financially destroy if my health-insuranceless body was taken over by cancer. Thankfully, I spotted Jocelyn seated—like an angel—near the back of the bus. She stayed there well after the initial crush of passengers moved forward. Jockeying for position was not her thing. I moved closer to the door as passengers filed off. They all looked beat.

"People are fucked," she said before her second foot touched the pavement. She was wearing the white linen pants. That meant a thong could be in my immediate future. We kissed.

"What happened?"

"Oh, boy, you're going to love this." She scanned the small crowd. "See dumpy-ass over there? With the Princess Leia haircut?"

The young woman in question was standing in a puddle of urine-colored light. Her billowing Sinbad pants and leotard top were chicken-broth green. She poked the pay phone dial pad like it was the chest of someone who had wronged her.

"Of all the fucking people, who do you think sat down next to me?"

"Nut job?"

"And, oh, my God, does she ever smell." Jocelyn gagged. A fake, but a nice touch.

"Onion pizza?"

"Worse. Halibut."

"Oh, man."

"I'm not kidding. I had to put Blistex on my nostrils. Feel."

I touched her mustache patch. It was still slippery. I felt a twinge in my dick.

"And that's not the best part."

"Lucky you."

"I make a special trip to the Strand to buy a book for the trip, right?" She drew a copy of Maxine Hong-Kingston's *Woman Warrior* from her pocketbook. "So as I'm smearing Blistex all over my face so I can read without puking, she sees the book on my lap and asks me if she can take a look at it because she likes the title."

"And you let her?"

"I didn't think she was going to read the whole thing."

"No shit."

"Can you believe that?"

"Did you tell her you wanted it back?"

"I couldn't."

"Why?"

"Because at first I thought she was just reading a few lines, you know? Then when she turned the page, I was thinking, There's no fucking way. And then, I'm not kidding, I was fascinated. What kind of person does that? I mean, to smell like that's one thing. Maybe she can't help it, you know? Some people smell. What can you do? But reading a stranger's book is just . . ." She shook her head, trying to jar the right word loose.

"Fucked up."

"Isn't it? And you know what she said when she gave it back? She said she was disappointed. She expected it to be different." Jocelyn's mouth was open wide with reenacted shock. "Can you fucking believe that?"

I took the book from her. "It's pretty thick. She's a fast reader." I spread the book open, raised it to my face, and took deep a whiff.

"I wouldn't."

"It smells like sea monkeys."

Jocelyn was entertained, but she acted like she didn't want to be. "You're sick."

"You're the one laughing, so what's that make you?"

"Sicker, probably."

The driver was pulling the last of the suitcases from the bus's lower compartment. Jocelyn took the opportunity to distance herself from the oddball sniffing the crotch of *The Woman Warrior*. I watched her walk. A thong it would be. She slipped the driver a couple bucks' tip.

"Why did you do that?" I said out of the corner of my mouth.

"Because that's what you do." Jocelyn's family was loaded and domestically disinterested enough to have their standing weekly grocery order delivered by a young man her mother described as a "nice colored fellow."

I took her bag, and we walked arm in arm in a line tangent to the rancid pool of light. "Go slow," I said. "I want to see if I can smell her."

"Stop."

I pulled Jocelyn closer to me. Princess Leia was giving the gears to whoever the poor fuck was that she'd called: "Do not fucking stand there and tell me you didn't tell me that."

Jocelyn squeezed my arm. "My God," she whispered, "look at the receiver." The cord leading to it was frayed and completely severed from the rest of the telephone.

"Do not humiliate me here," Leia said to her imaginary friend.

"Humiliate her somewhere else," I whispered.

Jocelyn nibbled my ear and told me I was a terrible person.

We walked toward my house along Pleasant Street. It was late June. Trustafarians with names like Zephyr, Flake, and Winnebago were reenacting scenes from *Billy Jack*, Burning Man, and Bread and Puppet on Amherst Common. They had established a tiny Hooverville of high-end pop tents, a small circular trampoline, and some anti-whatever signs. Someone was blowing a spastic tune on a flute. Two dudes were squeezing those long African drums Paul Simon had a total hard-on for around the time of the *Graceland* album. Birds from deep within the majestic, centuries-old elm trees were screaming like their throats were being cut.

"Fucking hippies," Jocelyn said, tapping into her mean streak. "Free Leonard Peltier, my fucking ass. These are the same assholes with No Blood for Oil bumper stickers."

"So?" I didn't particularly like hippies, but I didn't particularly hate them, either. Mostly they were invisible to me.

"So? So doesn't the bumper of a fucking Volvo seem like an odd place for that sentiment?"

"It's not like they're actually hurting anybody."

"What do you mean? That's exactly what they're doing. It makes me sick." She was getting heated up. I knew how little it would take for her to turn that heat directly on me.

"Hey," I said. "Guess who bought new sheets?"

"WHAT KIND OF film are we talking about?" I asked Marie.

"A documentary."

"Oh."

She laughed. "You seem disappointed. What did you think I meant, porn?"

"No."

Marie was loosening up. How loose remained to be seen. The waiter took his time placing two fresh drinks near the hub of the table. He was eavesdropping. I waited until he was gone before I spoke.

"I don't know if I have the head for any kind of work

right now," I said. "I'm in the middle of some heavy personal stuff."

"Who isn't?"

"I don't know. Lots of people?"

"I've never met any of them." Marie got to work on the new drink. "I'm not going to try too hard to convince you of what you're up for. You know better than anyone."

"What's the movie about? Cape Cod surf culture and tattoos? Shit like that?"

Marie's eyes were the color of a drunk-friendly Jack and Coke. Two lovely crow's-feet appeared at their corners when she smiled. "It's about my son. He drowned four years ago."

JOCELYN WAS IN the bathroom, caulking the edges around her diaphragm with spermicidal jelly. We had an understanding that her inserting it in front of me would have had the opposite effect of a good Degas painting of a peasant woman washing herself. Nothing like a lot of real-life bending, reaching, and determined lower-lip biting to empty the sails of all wind.

"What a pain in the fucking balls," she said, climbing into bed. "I should go back on the pill."

"Why don't you? Seems like it would be a lot easier."

She got annoyed with me, like going back on the pill was my callous and uninformed idea. "Because the pill fucks up your body. That's why. They don't even know what it does to you long-term. I might never be able to get pregnant."

"So?"

She gave me a dirty look.

"Fine," I said. "Let's keep doing what we're doing."

Jocelyn rolled onto her back in a huff and slapped the comforter with both hands. "Because I don't want to get pregnant now."

I went cold. "Did something go wrong in there?"

"No. Not any more than usual. It's not like I can stick my head up my twat to check the fit."

"I can go back to wearing a rubber, too, if that makes you feel any better."

She pooh-poohed that idea like I was, for the ump-teenth time, overlooking the obvious. "I can't feel any-thing with a condom. I have to be able to feel you. You, not an inner tube—or it doesn't work for me."

I could have put on three rubbers after a dip in hot par-affin and still would have been able to bust a quality nut. I moved into the fetal position and faced her side. "I know," I said. "It's a drag for me, too, if I can't feel you."

"GOD, THAT's really horrible," I said.

"The worst," Marie said.

"How old was he?"

"Almost three."

"What was his name?" I instantly felt bad for referring to her son in the past tense.

"Sidney. After my father."

"Man, that sucks."

Marie took a drag off her smoke and blew extra hard at the ceiling. She ground the butt to death in an ashtray fashioned after a ship's steering wheel.

I searched the compost of my past. No one really close to me had died. "My ex had a miscarriage."

Marie winced. "That's so sad."

"It was a lot harder on her than it was on me, to be honest."

"It's hard on everyone. Was she far along?"

"Not at all." I said it a little too easy-come-easy-go.

Marie thought I was trying to appear strong. "You shouldn't downplay your feelings. It's still devastating."

"It's nowhere near as bad as what you went through."

She couldn't bring herself to disagree with that. She treaded lightly. "Is that why it didn't work out with you and—"

"Jocelyn."

"Is that why?"

"Not exactly, but it didn't help, you know?"

Marie shook her head. She knew. But what she knew and what I knew were like apples and orangutans. "Were you guys married?" she asked.

"Mm."

"How long?"

"We were together for about three years."

"After Sidney died, Jason and I tried to hang on." She stared into her drink as she stirred.

"That sucks. How long's it been since you guys split up?"

"Two years ago July."

"What happened?"

"What do you mean, what happened?" I think she was having second thoughts about me.

"I mean, did it just—" I was going to say "die." "Did you stop loving each other?"

"No, but if we had a hundred years we wouldn't have been able to work back to zero."

"Sorry, I didn't mean to dig stuff up."

"You didn't. And anyway, I'd better be able to dig stuff up, right? Or this film is going to suck." She laughed like she'd just cracked a joke from her hospice bed. "Hey, at least I don't feel like killing myself anymore."

"That's good."

She scared me.

I HAD A terrifying flash of Roy falling off the back of a boat and flailing in the ocean during his last minute of life. I shook my head like it was an Etch A Sketch I was trying to erase. In reality, Roy was kicking up a storm in the car seat because he didn't want to leave me.

"More, more, more," he cried. It sounded like "Moe, moe, moe."

"It's okay, pal," I said through the driver's-side window. I'd walked James and Roy to the car without first putting on a coat. "You'll be back on Friday."

James corrected me. "Tomorrow. Tomorrow and Friday."

Two pinecones flammed against the hood of the Suburban like sparrows in a suicide pact.

"What time tomorrow?"

"Regular time, why?"

"I kind of have to be somewhere at eleven."

"Where?"

"I might have a job."

"You're shitting me?"

"No I'm not."

"Sonovabitch." James said. "Doing fucking what?"

"I don't want to say yet because I'm not sure if I have it, or if I even want it."

"Fucking fuck." He glanced in the rearview mirror to confirm that, yes, Roy existed. James was like a billion-dollar enterprise jeopardized by the failure of the three-dollar part. "Well, I hope you don't get the job."

"Thanks."

"Hey, I'm sorry, but if you can't watch the kid, I'm screwed. For real."

"I'll still watch Roy for you. It's only for a couple weeks, part-time."

"Is it close by? Can you tell me that much or is that some big fucking secret, too?"

"Yes, very close by."

"Hmm," he said, trying to reconcile numbers in his head.

"I swear, James, if the job starts to get in the way—"

"You're watching someone else's kid for money, aren't you?"

"Are you out of your mind? Look at me. I can barely keep myself clean."

He wasn't completely convinced.

"Dude," I said. "Me having a job is not going to be a problem. I give you my word."

"Well, I still hope you don't get it. These kind of things never go smooth."

"Jesus Christ."

"Well, they don't."

"I'll see you later. I'm freezing." I gave Roy two thumbs up, and started for the house.

"But what about tomorrow?"

I took a few more steps. I felt like sticking it to him a little bit. "What about it?"

"We on or what?"

"What do you think?"

"I thought we were on."

"We're still on."

"And don't forget, tonight's trash night."

· · ·

THAT NIGHT I collected my garbage. It all fit easily into a white plastic convenience-store bag that said Thank You three times in red.

"No, thank you. Really, I appreciate it." I tied a knot in the package. It looked like Johnny Appleseed's do-rag luggage. I should have been wearing a fucking pot on my head as I ran across the front lawn in my bare feet. The grass felt wet, but it was only cold. I put the bag at the curb. It looked like a widower's trash.

I went back inside and smoked in my bedroll. Marie had told me she was making the film of Sidney because every day she forgot more and more about him. I didn't know how making a movie was going to stop her from forgetting.

The next morning I looked out the window to see if my trash had been taken away.

Fuck me. I was becoming part of the order of things.

I BIKED OVER to Spunt's because I'd just wiped my ass with a coffee filter James had been using as a makeshift container for trim nails. It was a pleasant ride. Either I was creeping toward improved physical fitness or the bike was.

"Hey, Pay Phone," the kid with the pomegranate head said.

"Hey, Spunt."

He laughed like a three-year-old who thinks you think his name really is Tiger or Kiddo. "I'm no Spunt," he said.

"You sure look like one." I was in a good mood. I made myself a Coke Slurpee, then started tossing shit into a basket.

"Pay Phone, know what rhymes with *Spunt*?"

"I think so," I said over the Frito-Lay rack.

"*Runt*." He laughed. "Guess what else?"

"Well," I looked around. I couldn't resist. "There's *cunt*."

"That's what I was going to say." He cracked up. "*Cunt* rhymes with *Spunt*."

I heard a toilet flush. Tommy the cop walked out of the bathroom wearing street clothes, holding an *Auto Trader* magazine. He was a good cop. He made me instantly.

"Hey, hey, hey. It's the bike nut."

"Only on the side roads," I added.

"That's what we like to hear." Spunt had the hiccups from laughing. "What I miss?" Tommy asked as he put the magazine back on the rack. "Must have been a good one."

"Nothing," I said.

"This guy"—Spunt pointed to me—"this is a funny guy."

"Funny's good. Everybody likes a funny guy." Tommy grabbed two rival microwave burritos—one in each hand—and compared their weights. He flipped the loser back in the refrigerated case.

"Hey, Tommy?" Spunt broke into a football fight song: "Let's go Titans. Right?"

"I hear that, Ricky." Tommy opened the microwave door. It looked like a cat puked in it. "Big game Saturday." He pressed the start button and turned to me. "You going?"

"Where?"

"East Falmouth–Barnstable game."

"Hockey?"

"No," he whinnied. "Football."

"Yeah, I'm not much of a sports fan." I liked baseball and hockey, but only at the pro level. I'd rather watch two rutting bucks fight over a salt lick than a high school sport.

"Celts, Sox, Bs, Pats," Ricky raised a finger for each of Boston's major sports teams. "They are all awesome."

"Preview of the Cape Cod Conference Finals, you know," Tommy said, trying to sweeten the deal for me.

"Tommy, you see Bourque's goal last night?"

"Eff yeah, I did." Tommy turned back to me. "You'll be missing a primo game."

"Where's it at?" I asked.

"East Falmouth High. Less than a click from here." Tommy pointed out the window, as if East Falmouth High School were right there on the other side of his yellow Datsun B210 pickup.

"I don't know," I said, and took a pull off my Slurpee. "Maybe I'll check it out."

"We got this kid," Tommy said, "Whitman, a running

back. Can move the football. Runs like, whew." He slapped his hands together and sent the top one off like a shot. "Full boat to Notre Dame."

"Full boat," I said. "Good for him." I pictured this Whitman kid ten years down the road, divorced, two kids, installing urinating cherubs in the backyards of tacky Cape Cod Guinzos.

Tommy checked on his burrito, then keyed in some more time. "Deserves it, too. He's a good kid." He lowered his voice. "Black kid. Couple of them on the team. He's by far the best one. Don't get me wrong. I don't care if he's green."

"Tommy, Bird would have been the best ever— better than Dr. J and Magic—if it wasn't for his back, wouldn't he?"

"Not would have been."

"What do you mean?"

Tommy spelled it out for him. "Larry is the best of all time."

"I knew it," Ricky said. He could now scuttle off and settle a dispute. "What about the parade after they beat the Sixers?" Ricky asked. "Moses eats Bird shit," he chanted. "Moses eats Bird shit."

The microwave sounded. Tommy checked his burrito. "You got to do something about this oven." He went to straighten his cop utility belt, but he was wearing fleece sweats. They were maroon with gold piping. They looked so comfortable.

· · ·

MARIE'S LIVING ROOM was almost as spartan as my
sister's, but elegant. The floor was blond, satin-finished
hardwood. The walls were yellow. There were two
chrome-framed lounge chairs with painted pony-hide
seats, backs, and sides. They were worth more than me.
They faced each other, separated by a brass floor lamp
with a green glass shade and a coffee table that had been
an oxblood touring wardrobe in a previous life. That was
it for furniture.

"Mind taking your shoes off?" Marie was wearing a white
long-sleeve T-shirt. The frayed ends of her Levi's brushed
the tops of her bare feet. Her toenails were purple. I set
my shoes down next to her purple Doc Martens boots on a
woven palm-frond doormat. I was embarrassed because my
feet smelled.

"I used to have a pair of mustard-yellow Hush Puppies
loafers that made my feet reek," Marie said.

"Sorry about that."

"Don't be. I wasn't. They were my favorite shoes. I
wore them all the time anyway until my husband threw
them out."

I changed the subject. "This is a beautiful room," I said,
like I'd never seen it before.

"It's not bad." She looked around. "I think I'm going to
be ready to sell soon."

"Is this your house?"

"Mm."

"I'll never own a house. I just know it. I've never even owned a used car."

"You'd be surprised how fast things can fall into place. Out of place, too."

"Out of place I can relate to."

"One week I'm renting a slummy apartment in Central Square, next week I inherit a house on the Cape."

"That's pretty cool."

"I'd rather have my mother back."

I COULDN'T STOP singing the line "What's so bad about dying?" from the Plush tune "Found a Little Baby." It was driving Jocelyn crazy.

"Thanks," she said, without looking up from her *Harper's*. "I used to like that song."

"Sorry." I clammed up for about thirty seconds and resumed speed-reading Emerson's complete works from a cinder-block-sized *Norton Anthology of American Literature* open on my kitchen table.

I skipped right over Emerson and many like him when I was in college. I didn't want to go to grad school, but it was still a more appealing option than getting a job selling IRAs over the phone for Fidelity or hawking cases of fluoride treatment kits to dentists.

"What's so bad about dying?"

"Okay, I mean it now," she said sternly. "You really have to stop that."

"I can't help it."

"Try and help it."

I gave Emerson another go. He was making me sleepy. The GRE was the next morning at eight. I'd decided at the last minute to take it. I was cramming. It felt like not-so-old times.

I was applying to UMass and UMass only because I had some suck there with an English professor named Sanbourne. He was a middle-aged, brooding dude made of knotty pine and crooked teeth. He was the kind of guy you could easily picture cursing into John Berryman's *The Dream Songs*, getting shitfaced alone in a cabin after digging a new sump.

"What kind of suck?" Jocelyn asked, like I was full of shit.

"He told me I should apply."

"Just like that? 'You should apply'?"

"Pretty much."

"Hmm."

This was the extent of my suck: One morning before class a couple of us were smoking outside Bartlett Hall. Sanbourne didn't just bum a smoke. He bummed a brand. I gave him a Winston. Before flicking my Bic, he pointed it at me and said I should think about grad school.

"You'll see," Jocelyn said. "You will loathe grad

school." She was trying to sound like she'd given up long ago on trying to talk me out of it.

"We'll see." I began to sing the melody—sans lyrics—to the Plush tune.

Jocelyn slammed her magazine shut. "I cannot fucking fathom why you'd go through with this. Just go get a job. People do it all the time."

"You mean like you?" She rolled her eyes. "What, you think I'm wrong?" She didn't answer, so I gave her the other barrel. "I'm not the one who has the luxury of holding out for the coolest unpaid internship of my choice."

"Just because I have access to a little money doesn't—"

"Oh, right, a little money."

"It doesn't mean I'm wrong."

"Well, you know what? I have no money."

"Then, please, I'm begging you, let me give it to you. It kills me to watch you waste your life."

"I don't want your money." I did want it. But taking ten or twelve grand was a lot different from letting her pay for our dates and the odd weekend away. "I'd feel like a fucking loser."

"Okay, then, borrow it from me."

"We both know I'd never be able to pay you back."

"Then don't pay me back. I don't care about the money."

"*I* do. I'm not taking your money."

She led me onto thin ice. "If we were married, you'd take it, right?"

"Probably, but I'm not ready to get married." I was hoping she'd forgotten about the hundreds of times I'd proposed to her. That was before the infatuation started losing some of its sheen.

"Oh, I see."

I challenged her. "You see what?"

"Just read your fucking *Self*-fucking-*Reliance*."

WHEN I WOKE the next morning it was raining like a motherfucker. Jocelyn was hugging me like I was a body pillow. Each time I tried to slip away, she tightened her grip.

"Come on. Let me go." I was this close to blowing off the exam, but I'd already paid the fee.

"You're making a big mistake. Grad students are the worst kind of people."

I ended up regally shitting the bed on the literature subject exam. I did pretty good on the math and verbal. All told, I thought my scores were high enough to get me back into UMass.

I sent Sanbourne a letter at his sabbatical address in Caribou, Maine, letting him know my application package was in the system. The letter went unanswered. Even if he did flag my application, it didn't do me a fuck of a lot of good. That morning in front of Bartlett Hall, he must have been talking to the fucker who smoked Newports.

MOST OF THE FILMING WAS to take place in Sidney's old room. Marie led me into the small, dark hallway that ended at his closed bedroom door. She was telling me about some performance artist who had kept the packaging to every scrap of food he'd eaten over the course of a year. Fuck, I'd had roommates who did better than that without even trying.

"His whole thing is measuring intangibles against the refuse of what fuels it."

"Interesting," I said. "Was he German?" It was my way of indirectly asking if the performance artist had saved his shit and piss for the year.

"No, Japanese. Why? Have you heard of a German artist who has done something similar?" She seemed genuinely interested to know.

"I might have, but my memory's crap."

Marie had her hand on the doorknob. She went into deeper analysis of the Japanese dude's art. I started picturing mountains of plastic wrap and plastic foam trays soaked with blood from red meat, and crusty-mouthed chocolate milk cartons, and knotted condoms as stiff as potato chips.

She opened the door. "I wanted to do something in the spirit of that."

"Wow. That's a lot of stuff."

Sidney's room was an overflowing ten-by-ten purple box. It looked like someone had dumped the contents of a cargo net full of secondhand Save the Children relief.

"I trashed or gave away more than that." She sounded sorry that she hadn't kept every item—food, diapers, or otherwise—that Sidney had consumed during his short life.

Piles of entangled toys and clothes overran the floor like kudzu. There was hardly a place to stand. A white-barred crib was overpopulated with stuffed animals, like a pen used to turn calves into veal. More clothes and fleece baby blankets buried a toddler bed, like heavy snow on a car. Sunlight poured into the room through two sliding glass doors. A larger-than-life poster of a serious-looking Kermit the Frog watched over everything.

"I called a few of my girlfriends and got some of it back."

"You tell them what it was for?"

"The ones I thought would understand." She held up a tiny orange shirt with a purple dinosaur on it. "Some of the stuff, I'm not sure was ever ours." She refolded the shirt and put it back on the heap. "It's all here, though, because I can't be sure."

I looked out through the sliding glass doors. The small backyard sloped down and butted against the pond-calm water of Opal Cove. Somehow I was sure Sidney had drowned right there.

"So," Marie sighed, "there is a method to this madness." I was picturing Sidney running down the small hill to the water, unable to counter the deadly momentum that launched him out too deep. "I want to remove a little at a time until—by the end of the film—it will be just me sitting in this empty room."

I FELT PRETTY good when I woke up because it was exactly the kind of Saturday morning I loved as a kid: cold and gray. The first snow was still weeks away, but there was a sense that anything could happen. I turned on the TV and caught the tail end of a commercial for some acne scrub. Two pristine teenage couples were blasting around a California beach in a jeep, laughing at the funniest fucking joke ever told. The backing musical track was a note-for-note rip-off of the guitar lead in R.E.M.'s "Flowers of Guatemala." It started to piss me off, but then I watched some Looney Tunes. The new episodes—the ones without Mel Blanc doing the voices—were depressing, but they tossed in a vintage Bugs Bunny, the one set in ancient Rome. It lifted my spirits back up. I quoted Bugs Bunny while I showered.

When James and Dogshit showed up out of the blue, I was sitting on the porch, reading some film notes Marie had put together for me. I folded up the pages and hid them in my back pocket before they'd crossed the lawn.

"What's that?" James asked. "Employee handbook?"

"What's what?"

"I'm fucking with you." He laughed. Dogshit laughed,

too. "I don't care if it is. I thought about it. I'm cool with you working."

"Thanks, Dad."

Dogshit laughed at that, too.

James reached for the upper hand. "Even if you are going to pussy out and not tell anybody what exactly it is you're doing."

"Yeah, why's that?" Dogshit asked. "A job's a job, no?"

James gave wordless confirmation.

Dogshit continued. "I mean, I emptied Porta-Johns. I worked at the dump. I drove around for the MDC picking up roadkill and shit. I cleaned the wading pool at—"

James nudged me. "He found Sinn Fein dead on Twenty-eight," like I was supposed to know who or what the fuck Sinn Fein was.

"That was a harsh toke," Dogshit said. He swallowed uncomfortably. "One side of his head was caved in, and his tongue was really long and green. I had to wash the blood off his collar before I gave it back to Finneran."

"Harsh," James said. *Harsh* was the adjective of the moment for James and Dogshit. They used it without discretion. In a week or two, it would be *fierce*, *insane*, or *deadly*.

"I never told Finneran that part about his dog's head being mushed to a pulp."

"Why the fuck would you?"

"I wouldn't." There was a pause. "So what the fuck?" Dogshit asked me. "Who you working for?"

I told them.

"Well, that settles one thing," James said. "He's definitely not babysitting."

"Oh, man, that's harsh," Dogshit said. They both laughed.

"Seriously," James said, "what are you doing for her?"

"I'm helping her make a movie."

"What the fuck kind of movie?"

"You going to bone her?" Dogshit asked.

"It's a documentary. No, I don't think so."

"A documentary about what?"

"It's about her kid."

James shook his head. "Man, you really do have a dark streak running through you." He said it like he'd had more than one conversation behind my back on the subject.

"It's just a job," I said.

"No. What I have is just a job. Fixing boats is just a job."

"I don't know," Dogshit said. "Sounds kind of cool." James looked at him. "In a fucked-up way."

JAMES AND DOGSHIT convinced me to go with them to the East Falmouth–Barnstable game. If Minnesota is "the Land of Ten Thousand Lakes," then Cape Cod is "the Land of Ten Thousand Dunkin' Donuts." We hit one of them on our way to the game.

"Wouldn't it be cheaper if we all pitched in and bought a dozen instead?" Dogshit asked.

"Now you're thinking." James canceled his order.

The doughnut girl sighed. She tried to locate the void register key in a mug stuffed with pens, highlighters, and rubber bands. "Goddamnit." She emptied the mug onto the counter. A pen rolled onto the floor. I picked it up and placed it near the mug.

"How long till kickoff?" James asked.

"T minus five minutes," Dogshit said.

"Christ almighty. You want to just skip this shit and get something there?"

"Lines will be insane."

The girl hollered in the direction of the back room. "Who isn't putting the friggin' register key back where it goes?"

James looked at his watch. "This is pointless."

"Look," the girl snapped, "would you give me half a fucking second, please?"

James said something under his breath.

"What was that?" she asked. I looked at Dogshit, and he raised his eyebrows.

"I said, 'Take your time.' "

THE LOT at East Falmouth High School was full, and cars were backed up along Plymouth Street and its tributaries. We parked in Dogshit's cousin's driveway.

"What's his name?" I asked. "Apeshit?"

James laughed.

"Okay," Dogshit said, "I see how things are here. I was going easy on you because you're all fucked up, but no more." He challenged me to a slap boxing match. I wouldn't put up my dukes. He danced around me, then tapped me, unchallenged, on the cheek. "Down goes Frazier!" he said like Howard Cosell. "Down goes Frazier!" He put his arms up in victory and made crowd noises.

A real cheer erupted from inside Colonel James J. Sweeney Memorial Field.

"Come on, you homos. We just missed something."

The bleachers on both sides of the field were full, and fans stood three people-deep along the sidelines and behind the end zones. I assumed East Falmouth was the team in green and gold, since James and Dogshit instinctively moved to that side.

A man with an elfin voice yelled, "Hey, Jimbo!"

James was literally head and shoulders above most people standing. He scanned the crowd until he located the person attached to the voice. "Swainer!" James yelled. "You haven't been up this early since you were in high school."

People laughed.

"What do you mean 'up'?" Swainer said. "I ain't been to frickin' bed yet."

More laughs.

"Outstanding!" James said.

Another disembodied voice cheered for Swainer.

"Beers at the Nail after we KICK BARNSTABLE'S ASS!" Swainer yelled.

A cheer rose.

"We'll see, buddy," James said. "Now get a job." He gave Swainer a wide-handed wave. We worked our way close to the bleachers. Two kids standing on a scaffolding flipped the numbers on the scoreboard. We had missed most of the first quarter. East Falmouth was up, eight–zip. I couldn't give a fuck.

"How'd we score?" James asked a guy in front of us.

"Whitman, who else? Took it in from the eighteen. Then he got the conversion."

"Outstanding. Kid's on his way."

"If he can stay healthy," the guy said.

"And out of jail," someone else said.

"Harsh."

"Very harsh."

NEAR THE END of the second quarter I had to take a leak.

"I told you you should have used the can at Dunkin's. The Porta-Johns are horrible."

"Don't listen to him," Dogshit said. "They're fine."

"If I'm not back in a week . . ."

"Shit," James said. "I might as well go now and avoid the rush."

We walked under the bleachers. Kids were having a three-on-three touch football game.

"Someone's going to get mangled on all this glass," I said.

"That shit never happens."

As we passed the kids, James hijacked the play in motion by blocking the pass intended for a kid who was wide open.

"Down over!" the offended kid yelled. The two pipsqueak teams started arguing over whether or not the play counted.

"Fair's fair," James told them. "The play stands."

The kids screamed. People in the bleachers looked down to see what was up. Women closed their legs.

"Hey, it's Pay Phone." Ricky's upside-down head was looking at me from between his legs. So was Tommy the cop's.

"Couldn't stay away, could you?" Tommy asked.

"Guess not," I said.

"Where you sitting?"

I threw a thumb back over my shoulder.

"There's room up here," Ricky said.

"Squeeze down," Tommy told the people on the other side of Ricky.

"No, that's cool," I said. "I'm with some people."

"How many?" Tommy asked.

"Two."

"Gotcha," he said, like me giving my companions the slip and joining him was what I really wanted to do. "Next time we'll plan it out better." He saluted me and got back into the game. Ricky waved. James and I found the end of the shortest Porta-John line.

"How do you know that fuckwad?"

I knew he meant Tommy because James wouldn't make jokes about retarded people—mildly or otherwise. The story was sketchy, but someone in his family—a first or second cousin—had Down's syndrome. "Why's he a fuckwad?"

"Because I went to high school with his older brother. And that guy was a complete fuckwad."

"I CAN'T UNDERSTAND why you're friends with him," Jocelyn said. "Never mind live with him. That brings it to a whole other level of perplexing." She removed a cookie pan from the oven. On it were two small brown bowls of onion soup. A scab of mozzarella covered each.

"I could give you shit about some of your friends, but I don't because I don't let them bother me."

"You do give me shit about my friends."

"Like who?"

"Like Stephanie."

"Because she's a pain in the ass."

"Stephanie's nice."

"I can't fucking stand being around her."

"Because she's too New Agey for you. But she's a good person."

"I hate nurturers."

"She's helped me through a lot of stuff." Jocelyn made a face like it should be understood by both of us that I was to blame for a good deal of that "a lot of stuff" Stephanie had helped her through.

I mocked the look. "And Richie's helped me through a lot."

"You don't like Stephanie because she thinks crystals are magical. I don't like Richie because he's a dick." Jocelyn popped the tab on her can of diet Sprite. "Stephanie's a little out there. I'll give you that. She's not hurting anyone, though."

"Richie can be a very good guy."

"I'm sure. Even Hitler loved his dog."

"You're putting Richie and Hitler in the same group?"

She didn't answer.

"Give me a fucking break," I said. "You'll never like him because of Josie."

She swallowed her soda. "This is true. But I wouldn't have liked him anyway."

"You might if you got to know him." I peeled the cheese off the top of my soup. "If you saw his good side."

"You know what I can't fucking stand? That whole 'Such-and-such treats people like shit, but he's always been a good guy to me' mentality. It's fucking bullshit."

"God, you're really hard on people."

"I have to be. I'm sick of letting crap drift into my life."

"He likes you."

"Richie?"

"Yes."

"That's because I'm a good person."

"I mean he *likes* you."

"God help us."

MARIE FIXED A Fisher-Price pixel movie camera to a tripod in the middle of the bedroom. "I bought four of these right as they stopped making them."

"Is that a toy?"

"It was meant to be, but filmmakers discovered them."

"That's what you're going to film with?"

"Record with, technically." She opened the camera's cartridge bay, and slipped in a new Maxell audiocassette. "Pretty cool, huh?"

"How's it look?"

"Scrappy and beautiful."

"Color?"

"Better. Infinite analog shades of gray."

I did some quick math in my head: a case of cassette tapes, a toy camera, maybe some batteries. "So this is a big-budget picture."

She laughed. "Colossal. Actually, you're by far my biggest expense."

MY JOB WAS to interview Marie, asking her questions from a script she'd written. She wanted me to be positioned right behind the camera the whole time.

She said she hated it when she watched a documentary and the person on screen wasn't looking her in the eyes. She said that happened all the time. I'd never really noticed.

"How great would it be to have one of those contraptions Ross McElwee used in his films?" she asked.

"That would be amazing." I had no fucking idea what she was talking about.

Marie was sorting through a large manila envelope of colored, translucent lens filters, trying to determine which was appropriate. "Did I say Ross McElwee? I meant Errol Morris."

"Right."

"It's a pretty ingenious solution to the whole eye-to-eye thing. I can't believe it took so long for someone to come up with it."

I didn't say anything.

Marie stopped what she was doing and looked at me. "You have no idea who Errol Morris and Ross McElwee are, do you?"

"Not really."

"Why didn't you just say so?"

"I don't know. It's a bad habit."

She could have made me feel like a shit heel, but she didn't. "Isn't it weird how people do that?" she asked. "I've never read *The Great Gatsby*. Or *The Old Man and the Sea*. Whooptie-doo-shit."

I laughed. "Even I've read those."

"Yeah, but you don't know who Errol Morris is."

"Or Ross McEwen."

"McElwee. Ross McElwee."

"Fine. Ross McElwee."

Marie looked at her watch. "Okay. You're coming with me." She took my hand and led me out of Sidney's bedroom and into her own. She pushed me into a worn armchair next to her bed. "You stay there," she ordered. She went into her closet and emerged with a videocassette. She fired up the large television on top of her dresser and slid the tape into the VCR. She got prostrate, with her chin resting on a two-pillow stack at the foot of the bed. "If you don't like this, you're fired."

We watched *Gates of Heaven* and *Vernon, Florida*. Between films, Marie put two frozen pizzas in the oven. We drank a few beers. It was getting dark outside by the time we finished. I told Marie I thought both films were amazing. I could tell she was glad I got it.

"But if I had to choose I'd pick *Vernon, Florida*."

"Who is asking you to choose?"

LOU BARLOW FROM Sebadoh was headlining, playing solo acoustic, so I was okay with suffering through the four opening acts. One of them was Jocelyn's friend Stephen's band. They were called the Coughins. They all smoked onstage and went to great lengths to look like they couldn't give a shit how they looked. They embraced the crappy-playing-equals-pure-art-and-unmolested-genius myth. Stephen graduated from Pratt, but was doing production at *Redbook* because it was easy money. Jocelyn said that he'd designed some nice Vera Wang bridal knockoffs, and too bad they were counterfeits. I wasn't too impressed, since Stephen had merely copied Vera's design. Jocelyn said it still wasn't easy to do. She suggested I try banging out a Cézanne.

Stephen put us on the Coughins' guest list. The whole band probably only got two guests, so I was grateful. I liked Lou Barlow's songs a lot. I wasn't alone. When dangerously full, Brownies held about two hundred and fifty people. All three nights sold out in about twelve seconds.

After the Coughins' set of Game Theory B-sides, Jocelyn and I went outside to have a smoke and wait for Stephen. It was one of the first nice nights in April, when you think you might actually live to see the summer. A crowd of people kept us from venturing too far beyond the entrance. Two bouncers stood like enormous African urns on either side of the doorway

One of them got up on a milk crate and made an announcement. "People, the show is sold out. If you don't have tickets, go somewhere else. I repeat. The show is sold out. Sorry."

People moaned, though very few left.

"You're not sorry," the other bouncer joked.

"You're right. I don't give a flying fuck who they do or don't let in. Let 'em all in. Let none of 'em in. I don't care." They laughed.

"I like these guys." Jocelyn said about the bouncers, loud enough for them to hear.

"You catching that?" one of the bouncers asked.

"Oh, yeah." He called in to the guy taking tickets. "Zippy? Zip, you make sure this pretty lady and her friend get treated nice."

"What's that?" Zippy was flustered, taking tickets like a madman and trying to make sense of a messy guest list. Brownies was not accustomed to crowds this size.

"Forget it, Zip. Go back to work." The bouncer winked at Jocelyn.

"Zipper-headed Zippy," said the other.

Two sonic youths wormed up to the front of the line. "You sure there aren't any more tickets?" one of them asked.

"One moment, please." The bouncer got back up on his milk crate. "Oh, I forgot to mention," he screamed down at the sonic youths. "The show is sold out! Go home!"

People with tickets laughed. The bouncer stepped off the crate. The sonic youths evaporated.

Stephen finally came outside. He'd changed into a ratty white T-shirt that said "Be All You Can Be." His hair was wet, and his face was red. He was hyper and effeminate.

"Hey, you!" He hugged Jocelyn. Then he hugged me. I wasn't into it. I don't like people who I'm not fucking touching me. "How were we? Be honest."

"You looked like you were having a good time up there." It was the most positive thing I could come up with.

"Really? Thanks." He was still breathing heavy from the gig.

"I agree," Jocelyn said. "You guys were amazing."

"Thanks, you guys." He group-hugged us.

"Nice set," someone leaving the club said.

"Thank you soooo much."

"Was it good for you?" Jocelyn asked.

Stephen turned into Willona, the lusty neighbor on the TV show *Good Times*. "Sister, it's always good for me." Jocelyn slapped him on the arm. "No, there were some bumps, you know? But on the whole, I think it was—no, I know it was our best show yet. Each one gets better." Stephen moved his hand in small increments from the left side of his body to his right, mimicking the Coughins' evolution as a band. "And as long as that keeps happening, you know?"

"Something good's got to happen," Jocelyn said.

"Improvement's what you want," I said.

"That's what I keep telling Jeremy, but he's so"— Stephen clenched his fists—"he wants everything to happen yesterday. He's like a child. But you know what? I'm not going to think about his issues tonight. This is me not thinking about it. It was our best show yet, and I'm going to enjoy it."

"You go, girl," Jocelyn said.

The Coughins were never going anywhere, and at least two of the three of us knew it.

The crowd in front of Brownies parted. Lou Barlow waited while the rest of his party got out of the cab. He looked like a Lovin' Spoonful–era John Sebastian. There was a scrawny dude wearing an unfashionably full beard and an olive drab army fatigues jacket. He had a camera in his hands, and two more around his neck. He immediately swapped out lenses. A green-haired woman wearing a co-opted auto mechanics jacket with LADY SUB POP embroidered in pink on a breast pocket was reading the number off her pager.

"Lou's here!" people murmured. "That's him."

Lou walked the length of the concrete-gray carpet. He saw Stephen standing near the door.

"Hey, man. Sorry I missed your set. Fucking ridiculous photo shoot."

The photographer was unfazed. He got the camera right up in Lou's face.

"Oh, please," Stephen said. "Thanks for just letting us play."

"Was anyone there?"

"By the end it was pretty full. More people than we've ever played to."

"Cool."

Stephen introduced us. He told Lou I lived in Amherst.

"Yeah, you look kind of familiar," Lou said.

"I wait tables at that restaurant, Esposito's." I had also seen Dinosaur Jr. play about twenty times when he was still in the band. I left out that part because I didn't think it was a good idea stirring up the bad blood.

"He's got a cool band, too," Stephen said. "The Young Accuser."

"Cool."

I was embarrassed. "It's not really a band. Just me and another guy on acoustics. I think you know him. Richie Leonides?"

"No way! *The* Richie Leonides? He's a musician?"

"Sort of."

"I worked with him in the kitchen at the Soldiers Home in Holyoke."

"Yeah, I know."

"Fuck! That was like 'eighty-two, 'eighty-three. He's the guy that got me way into Sabbath."

"No way!" Stephen said. "He's the one?"

"Totally. I owe that guy a lot." And with that, Jocelyn added Lou Barlow to her shit list. "He also showed me how to suck the nitrous out of these big industrial canisters. I definitely owe him a lot."

Lady Sub Pop finished sorting out arrangements with Zippy the doorman.

"Okay," she said, "they'll let us use the upstairs office

for the interviews, but we have to do them, like, right now."

"Fuck," Lou sighed. "All of these fuckers think they own you."

Lady Sub Pop took Lou's disdain for her and her industry as a healthy and highly marketable display of indie cred. She nudged the photographer back to work.

I sheepishly took a three-song cassette from my pocket. "You don't have to listen to it, but maybe you could pass it on to your guy at the label."

"That would be me." Lady Sub Pop accepted the tape like a mother into whose hand a child spits his spent chewing gum. The scrawny dude photographed the whole thing. I pictured my demo suspended in a pillar of wet paper towels, lipstick-kissed Kleenex, and feminine-hygiene packaging in the ladies' room trash can.

LOU'S SET WAS very good. He tried out some new songs and a bunch of my favorites off *The Freed Weed*. Jocelyn and I got moderately shitfaced. Except for two guys who chose a Lou Barlow acoustic set as background music for their five-year high school reunion, the room was dead quiet when he played. People shushed them with little lasting effect. Lou finally stopped a few bars into "Soul and Fire" and told them to get the fuck out. The audience cheered. Lou shaded his eyes from the stage lights and scanned the crowd.

"I'm serious," he said. "Get the fuck out! Get your ten bucks back—or however the fuck much it is—and get the fuck out!"

The audience went crazy. We all started chanting, "Get the fuck out!" The two guys got the fuck out. One of them held the bird high like he was carrying the Olympic torch.

"Fucking maggots," Lou said, then started the tune from the top.

AFTER THE GIG, we hung around and had a few drinks at the bar with Lou. Only musicians and their satellites remained in the club. We were talking about Robin Williams, trying to estimate how much cocaine—both in weight and in money—he'd done behind the scenes of *Mork and Mindy*. The amounts varied greatly, but even the lowball figure was a lot. We agreed that however much it was, it was more than any of us had done. We toasted to that.

It came up that Fifi had recently opened some Sebadoh shows in Holland and Germany. Stephen told Lou that Jocelyn and Roger Lyon III had a past—a very brief past.

Lou didn't hold back. He said Roger Lyon III was a dick for a number of reasons. "He'd sing a line and then spit all over the place."

I loved it. I had to know more. "What do you mean, by accident?"

"Fuck, no." Lou imitated Lyon III flapping his phlegmy epiglottis.

"Gross," Stephen said.

"And he kept spitting through their entire set."

"Did he spit on the audience?" I asked.

"On the audience, on the stage, on the monitors, on the amps. It was fucking weird."

"What's the point?"

"Exactly." Lou scraped the soles of his shoes on a bar-stool rung. "I had to wade through his fucking throat eggs every night."

"Eww. That's so gross," Stephen said.

"I was like, 'Dude, someone's going to get sick from all that saliva and phlegm.' And he says, 'What are you talking about?'"

"What a fucking dick," I said.

Lou turned to Jocelyn. "How long were you his girlfriend?"

Jocelyn was not completely immune to being star-struck, or she never would have gone out with Lyon III in the first place. If Lou Barlow had been Joe Public, she would have told him it was none of his fucking business. "We went on three dates."

I added color. "And the first one was when he picked her up after one of his shitty band's shitty shows."

"He's got that down to a science these days," Lou said. He put his hand on my shoulder. "I don't know jack shit about this guy right here, but I'm sure he's a huge upgrade from Roger Lyon the Fucking Third. A huge upgrade."

"And what kind of pretentious fuckwit puts 'the Third' at the end of his name?" I asked.

"An enormous one."

Lady Sub Pop was sitting alone near the low stage, patiently bored stiff, drinking a can of Diet Coke. She was ready to go back to her chrome room at the Paramount an hour before.

Lou called to her, "Jenna, from now on I want to be called Lou Barlow the Third."

Jenna smiled, using the last of her A&R man's daily allotment of phony amusement.

"No, even better, Lou Barlow Junior." He stood on the rungs of his bar stool and proposed a toast to his new name.

JOCELYN TOLD OUR cabbie we were going to Brooklyn. He groaned like he'd just been told by his boss that he was going to have to take a small pay cut.

"Sorry"—Jocelyn looked at the cabbie's nameplate display— "Ahmed, but that's where I live."

I gave her a look.

"Don't look at me like that," she said. "They have to take you."

I was not so drunk that I couldn't sense the eighth day of the Seven Days' War dawning. I distracted Jocelyn by pulling her closer to me on the slippery vinyl seat. I kissed her neck. Ahmed hauled ass toward Houston Street.

"And take the Manhattan Bridge, not Brooklyn," Jocelyn added for good measure.

Ahmed's eyes tightened in the rearview mirror.

The cab crossed the bridge the way a hovercraft does gentle sea swells. Jocelyn had her head tilted back far enough to look straight up through the rear windshield. Her tongue and teeth glistened. A sparse constellation made up almost entirely of aircraft shone through the blurry rhythm of ironwork. She started imitating the in-cab recording of Elmo telling tourists to buckle up and not to forget their shit when they left. I kissed her exposed throat.

She giggled.

The sound of the steel-belted radials on the road changed from a sizzle to a wash as the Manhattan Bridge became Flatbush Avenue.

"I like that Lou Barlow," I said.

Jocelyn had no comment. She lifted her ass off the seat and guided my hand under it before sitting back down. Traffic started backing up right around Junior's cheese-cake restaurant.

"Elmo says, 'Keep doing that.' "

"LOOK, ROY," James said, "it's Ron Jeremy, the king of hardcore!"

"James, if you only knew."

"As if."

"Listen. What do you think about me dropping you off at work so Roy and I can go somewhere in the truck?"

"Like where?"

"I don't fucking know. Isn't there a mall or a playground near the boatyard? It's just getting old going up and down this street all the time. I think Roy needs more stimulation."

James was suspicious. "Can you even drive?"

"Of course I can drive."

"I mean legally?"

As we pulled into the boatyard, Dogshit and two other scruffy-looking guys were drinking coffee and smoking alongside a long elevated red hull.

James let go of the steering wheel and rubbed his hands together like a miser. "That big red bitch is going to cover my nut till Christmas."

I had one hundred fifty dollars in my pocket Marie had paid me for my first three days of work. I was feeling pretty good about it. I was going to treat Roy to a grilled cheese or something. "How much you make on a repair like that?"

"Oh, you know," James said, "a gentleman never fucks and talks." He reached back over the front seat and grabbed a cooler from the floor. "Does he, sonny boy?"

Roy giggled.

James reluctantly dropped the keys into my hand. He

checked to make sure Dogshit was still way out of ear-shot. "You and I both know I don't even have to say it." He said it anyway. "I depend on this truck, so don't drive like a Chink."

The steering wheel was miles away. So were the pedals. I reached down and found the seat-adjusting lever. I couldn't release it. James was watching me. He came back to the Suburban and opened the driver's door.

"What the fuck's the problem?" Dogshit and the other guys looked on.

"I can't get it to——"

"Look out." James released the lever with one hand and moved the massive bench all the way forward with the other. "Close enough for you?"

It was too close, but I told him it was fine.

"And make sure you're back here by three sharp."

I unintentionally did a mini peel-out in a patch of sand. Roy loved it. I looked in the rearview mirror, and James was shaking his head.

I turned on the heater. The sweet smell of rotting tree waste blowing from the vent was nauseating. Roy was making a face like he'd just eaten a bad blueberry. I shut the heater down and opened a window. I was colder than I'd been three minutes earlier.

"What do you say we put some food in the furnace, Roy old kid?"

It was still too early for lunch, so I swung through

the McDonald's drive-through and bought a couple number-three breakfast combos. I got one with a coffee, and the other with the orange juice. I was planning on drinking both, but Roy spotted the orange juice from way the fuck back there in his car seat. He went completely batshit when I told him the sippy cup of lukewarm two-percent milk was all his. There was no reasoning with him. My options were to endure the tantrum or give in.

"Fine. Fine." I knew he couldn't help himself, but it still sucked getting yelled at. "Hang on." I held the orange juice between my knees while I drove and used a coffee stirrer to poke a small hole in the foil. He sucked on it and was instantly relieved, like the Levy character in *Marathon Man* when Zell, the Nazi sadist, rubs a numbing tincture of clove on the tooth he'd just drilled. "Is it safe, Roy? Is it safe?"

He glared at me while sucking away.

James had assured me there was no way it was going to rain. I pulled into the parking lot of the John Glenn Middle School and let Roy loose. The playground was a lot closer to the building than it looked from the road. A window of the classroom nearest the swing set had two crude gender representatives painted on it: a football and a horse with a pink mane. I could see the faces of kids dying at their desks. The teacher was a middle-aged woman. She was startled when she turned and saw me standing so close to the other side of the glass. I waved to her, one caretaker to another. She started to wave back, but stopped herself.

"We're not hurting anybody, right, Roy?" I pulled my knit hat from my pocket and concealed my homeless-guy hairdo. I showed off some fatherly affection by kissing Roy's cheek, then looked back into the classroom. I felt so sorry for Roy. He had his whole life ahead of him.

The playground was built for kids much older than Roy, so I had to sit on the swing and hold him in my lap. He didn't like it at first, but as soon as we started moving, everything was fine. It was kind of nice holding on to him. His fat fingers were white from squeezing the iron chains. He laughed more and more the higher we went.

I glanced into the classroom. The teacher was now talking to a man who resembled the father on the show *Family Ties*. I could see yellow in his beard. They exuded the same kind of distrust. They had me made for a pedophile fishing for a keeper, using little Roy as bait. I swung him less high. He wanted to get down and run around, so I let him.

"Careful, Roy. Careful."

He was standing in a depression worn into the ground, fucking around with the swing. I tried to pick him up and move him somewhere safer, but he screamed. Both teachers looked at me, so I left him where he was. He pushed hard on the swing. It came back and smashed him in the mouth. I knew he was going to cry like a motherfucker because for the first few seconds he made no sound at all. He just looked like he was screaming.

I picked him up and hugged him while he wailed. He was touching his mouth. His top lip was already swelling. I lifted it. One of his front teeth was outlined in a fine bead of blood. I touched the tooth, and he screamed. It was loose. I rocked him back and forth. His arms were so tight around my neck, I could have let go of him, and he would have stayed attached to me. I kissed his face and told him it would be okay. I gave him a drink of milk from his sippy cup. That calmed him. He left some bloody, milky drool around the mouthpiece. Seeing that almost broke my heart.

I sat back on a swing and tried to seat him on my lap, but he wanted me to hold him. He rested his head on my shoulder. I put my hand under the back of his coat. My fingers played over his ribs. It scared me to think of how easily they could be broken. I gently rocked us without taking my feet off the ground.

I wondered if Marie's son, Sidney, had been more or less afraid while dying than Roy was just then. Or are dying and a shocking whack in the mouth one and the terrible same when you don't know any better? I protected Roy with my body, but no one can protect someone forever.

Both teachers were watching from right up against the window.

"He's okay, for fuck's sake."

· · ·

WHEN WE PICKED James up at the boatyard, I told him right away about Roy's accident. James almost seemed excited to see the wound.

"Let's see that wobbly Chiclet." Roy resisted, but not enough. "Oh, you're okay. You'll live to get married."

"You think it's still in there good enough?"

"That thing's not going anywhere." It was one of the few times I was glad James was a know-it-all. "I'll tell Pamela I walked into him, just in case."

James asked for his car keys by sticking out his hand, palm up. "I tell you what, though. I don't know what the fuck we're going to do when Roy starts talking for real."

We stopped at Spunt's on the way home.

"Awesome football game," Ricky said, like I'd played a key role in East Falmouth's victory. He was wearing an enormous Boston Bruins home jersey. He looked like he'd been born without hands. "I've been waiting for you to come in. I got you something."

"For me?" I asked.

James was drinking from a quart of milk, watching us. Ricky reached into his hip pocket and removed a twenty-dollar prepaid telephone card, still in the cellophane wrapper. It had pictures of flags on it.

"So you won't need to change dollar bills into change to use the pay phone."

I was touched. "Oh, man, you got to let me pay for that."

"Why? It's prepaid."

"I don't know what to say."

James did, I'm sure. I could see him composing a string of homophobic cut-downs he would have delivered with relish if Ricky had been merely stupid.

Ricky showed me the price breakdown on the back of the card. "See? Six cents a minute. Now look." He raced over to the phone card display and came back with both a five-dollar and a ten-dollar card. He turned them over on the forest green Formica counter. "Seven cents a minute. And eight cents a minute." He raised the twenty-dollar card and exclaimed to the room, "This one's got the value."

James nodded in agreement, then polished off the quart of milk.

Roy was trying to lift a gallon jug of blue windshield-washer fluid.

WHILE JAMES GASSED UP the Suburban, I slipped out to the phone booth and test-drove my new phone card. I used a nickel to scrape off the scratch-ticket coating that concealed my access number. I jumped through the dialing hoops, then punched in the main number for *Redbook*. I had 325 minutes available for the call. I dialed Jocelyn's extension, and again I was rerouted to the receptionist.

"I'm sorry, she's no longer employed by *Redbook*."

"What do you mean?"

"She doesn't work here anymore."

"You're kidding? Since when?"

The receptionist went into protection mode. "I'm sorry. I can't say."

"Did she ever come back from her honeymoon?"

"Sir, I really can't—"

"You can't or you won't?"

"Is there someone else you'd like to speak to?"

"Joff."

"Who?"

"Joff Something-or-other."

She humored me and searched the directory. "I'm afraid there's no one named Joff working here, either."

I hung up and dialed Jocelyn's apartment. Still no answer. Still no answering machine. I bludgeoned the telephone with the receiver, then started walking back to the Suburban.

Jocelyn could have been anywhere: languidly drifting past a Grecian island with a Moroccan financier named Sergio or buying a box of fucking Spic and Span at the C-Town on Ninth Street. Maybe Roger Lyon III flew her over to meet up with the Australian leg of the Fifi tour, or some fucking shit like that. Lyon III seemed like just the type of strategically neglectful, dashing egomaniac who could bring a high-strung girl like Jocelyn around.

James stopped tapping his watch when he saw my face. I opened the passenger door.

He spoke over the top of the truck. "What happened to you?"

"What a fucking mess."

James smiled. He enjoyed that he understood all too well. "What she say?"

"Nothing. I can't reach her. It's like she disappeared."

"Good. Talking to her's the worst fucking thing you could do." He slapped the roof. "No. Seeing her is the worst thing." He started imitating the "weaker" sex, whichever sex that was. " 'Maybe we should meet for a coffee and just talk.' Next thing you know, you're caught—balls deep—back in the penis flytrap. Fuck that."

"I know, but it's fucking hard," I said.

"Damn straight, it's hard. But you have to be tough. What did Ronnie say, 'We don't negotiate with terrorists.' "

"I thought Reagan did negotiate with terrorists."

"Depends on who you ask. All I'm saying is, you talk to her, and just like that, you're set back months."

"I know, but—"

"Like in AA, when they give you a badge for every week you're dry. That's all fucking good and well, but you fall off the wagon, and those badges don't mean shit."

"What if you're meant to be a drunk?"

"I don't know. I guess, be a good one."

A pristine navy blue Chevy Impala from the early seventies pulled up on the other side of the pumps.

"Here comes Mr. Fucking Magoo," James said. "This is all I need." An elderly man got out and squinted at the gas prices. "How are you today, Mr. Mahoney?" James called over.

"Fine." It took Mr. Mahoney a few seconds to process just who James was. "Jimmy. I didn't recognize you."

"It's the gray hair." James took off his hat and slicked back his temples.

"I don't see any gray."

"Oh, it's there."

"Least you still got some." Mr. Mahoney ran his hand over his bald head. It was as shiny as a priest's.

They chuckled, each pretending to know the mythical inner peace that's supposed to come to aging men.

Mr. Mahoney grabbed a small, triangular wooden block from his dashboard. He slid the nozzle into his gas tank, then wedged the block into the nozzle's handle so he could fuel up hands free. "How are your mom and dad?"

"They're doing great," James said. "Thanks."

"That's fantastic. Give them my best."

"I certainly will. And give mine to Mrs. Mahoney."

"It's a deal." The old man walked toward the store, leaving the rigged pump unattended and racing toward a potential overflow.

When the coast was clear, James removed the block of wood and tossed it in the trash. "That man should not be allowed to drive." He finished filling Mahoney's tank the old-fashioned way. "No shit, they should retest all of them at sixty-five."

JAMES'S MOTHER DIED of bone cancer a few weeks after Roy was born. I went to her wake. It was open-casket. She looked like that nineteenth-century sailor they found preserved in a block of Arctic ice. I never met his father. He died not long after James and Pamela started dating. He was out fishing alone in his boat, and he had a stroke. They said he wouldn't have lived even if he'd had the stroke in the emergency room of Mass General. That made everyone feel better.

"PRETTY COOL, HUH?" I said. "A twelve-inch, stainless-steel skillet with an aluminum sandwich bottom."

"What do you know about aluminum sandwich bottoms?" Jocelyn said snidely. "You read that off the box."

I knew when I saw my mother's return address on the package that Jocelyn was going to have an issue with what was inside—whatever it was. I didn't feel like getting into it with her. We stood in my kitchen looking at the new skillet gleaming on my dulled, shit brown electric stove.

Jocelyn shook her head like something was a crying shame. "And she sent that to you out of the blue?" She knew damn well where it came from.

"Yup."

"That's weird."

"It's a fucking gift from my mother."

"It's more complex than that."

"Oh, it is?"

"Yes. I see it clear as day. Obviously you don't."

"Give me a break. Can't my mother buy me a pan?"

"It's the only pan you own."

"It's not my only pan."

"Correction: It's the only usable pan you own. I wouldn't wash my feet in your cookware."

"They're not that bad."

Jocelyn skipped right over the sorry state of the rest of my pots and pans. "She's still taking care of you. And you let her."

"That pan is taking care of me?"

"If you can't see that, then I don't know what to tell you."

Jocelyn's mother was a sclerotic-livered concern-sponge, the Bizarro World opposite of my own. Right then I felt like rubbing her nose in it, but that would have been cruel. So I rubbed her nose close to it. "You sure you're not just a tiny bit jealous?"

MARIE WAS SITTING in a folding chair. A threadbare, stuffed Hamburglar character with a broken neck was slumped over in a high chair next to her. It was so grim I wondered whether she had put him that way on purpose. The camera was rolling. I read from the script.

"Do you think you were ever going to tell Sidney he was an accident?"

"When he got old enough to understand, I would have. And I would have told him that sometimes an accident can be the best thing that ever happens to a person. It was for me." She took a drag off her smoke. "I thought about this a lot when he was alive. The only other thing that might possibly have changed me as profoundly as having him would have been surviving a life-threatening illness. New job, new city, marriage, divorce—even the death of my mother—didn't change me as much." She took another drag. "Before I had Sidney, I was a lot of things: selfish, vain, careless with other people's feelings. If it wasn't for him, I know I'd still be that old person. Maybe worse." She told me to stop shooting. "Fuck."

"What is it?"

"I don't like how I said that. Sounds so fucking fake."

I agreed, but didn't say so.

"I don't want to talk about it. Can we please just do another take, quickly, please?" She asked like I'd been trying to dissuade her.

"Sure. We can do as many as you'd like."

"What I'd like is to do one fucking good one. Again, please."

I rolled tape and we started over. I tried to sound more casual.

Marie left a pregnant pause between the question and her answer. "Sidney's father and I weren't married until after Sidney was born. I messed around on him before that. I loved him. It was shitty of me. I was young, stupid . . . Fuck, fuck, fuck, stop the fucking tape, please."

I stood up. Marie smashed her two fists together. "This sounds so retarded. Jesus fucking Christ." She mocked herself. " 'I was young, stupid.' Give me a fucking break. What is this? *How Green Was My Valley*?"

"I don't know that movie, but I'm sure you weren't that bad."

"Goddamnit, I wrote it exactly the way I wanted it, but it sounds like crap. I'd puke if I had to watch a film like that."

"Maybe you should just wing it." I knew what I was talking about. I had a lot of experience at going into something unprepared.

"How so?"

"I don't know. Why don't we just let the camera roll and shoot the shit."

A soft lightbulb went on inside her head. "Instead of act."

"Might feel better."

"I don't know. I spent a long time preparing. I had it all planned out. The look, the script, everything."

"You're the one who said sometimes an accident is the best thing. Did you mean that?"

Joe Pernice

224

"Yes."

"So?"

She positioned Hamburglar so that his head would remain upright. "That means I'm going to need something to sip." She got up and headed out of the room.

I called after her. "What are you having?"

"Bourbon."

"Set me up, too, would you?" I lit a cigarette and stood between the camera and the sliding glass doors. There was a spade sticking out of a weedy pile of loam off to one side of the backyard. I breathed on the glass, drew a triangle, then wiped it clean. "What in the fuck am I doing here."

"What was that?"

"Just thinking out loud." I turned. Marie was now in the doorway holding two coffee mugs of bourbon on ice. She gave me my drink, then checked to see if the camera was still in focus.

"Hey, you never turned off the camera," she said.

"I thought I did." I started for it. "I can just rewind it to where—"

"No, no, no. Don't bother. It's all part of the process." She sat back down in her chair. "As embarrassing as it may be." She raised her glass to me.

I got behind the camera. "You, as my mother would say, like to take drink, don't you?"

Marie laughed. "Now and then."

"Did you drink while you were pregnant?"

"Jesus, no. I quit everything—drinking, weed, cigarettes, coffee—all the things I'd tricked myself into believing weren't that bad for me. That's how I knew I was pregnant. Just imagining myself taking a sip of booze or coffee would make me retch. It's pretty remarkable when you think about it. There I was, a grown woman being watched out for by an embryo."

"Like all kinds of choices were being made for you."

"More like, all of a sudden, a lot of the things weren't even on my radar anymore. It was a relief. All the guilt, all the excuse making—gone. Replaced by the purpose of growing and delivering this person. It was very peaceful."

"Sounds pretty good."

"It wasn't pretty good. It was fucking amazing. And it kept getting better, especially after he was born. Who knows if it ever would have plateaued."

"Growing up, did you ever imagine having a kid could make you feel that good?"

"God, no. I never wanted kids. I remember when I was about twenty, my friend Tina taking my hand and placing it on her stomach when the baby was kicking. I didn't like it all. It just seemed creepy and wrong. She was way overdue, and her skin was pulled so tight, I thought her stomach was going to split open right there on the subway. It was disgusting. She got mad at me for saying so.

"But when I got pregnant, I loved it when Sidney woke

me up kicking. I'd just lie there in the dark with my hands on my stomach. I wouldn't even wake up Jason because I was worried that if I did, all the commotion would make the baby stop." Marie stared silently into the camera for a few seconds.

"Do you ever worry, like, okay, here was this great person who changed you and your whole world and everything, and now that they're gone, everything will go back to the shitty way it was before?"

"Obviously." She raised her mug of bourbon in one hand, and her smoke in the other. "But in other ways, it changes you for good. It stains you. I mean, look at me."

"Did you get all of those tattoos after he was born?"

"The better ones."

"Can I see?"

"Oh, God, really?"

"If you don't want to . . ."

"No. I do." She took off her shirt. It didn't seem like she was wearing just a bra because she was covered in ink. She tapped the place above her left breast. "This one . . ."

I couldn't make it out. "What is it?"

"Two dates. The day he was born and the day he died." She tapped the corresponding spot above her other breast.

"And that one?"

"Two more dates. My birthday and the day I was planning on killing myself."

. . .

BY THE END of the day's shoot, we were both frazzled. Marie thought we were onto something. I had a headache and I was starving. I asked her if she wanted to get something to eat, but she said she was too torched. She paid me another fifty bucks in cash and handpicked a few articles of clothing from a pile on the toddler bed.

"Here," she said. "These look like they'd be about Roy's size."

ROY WAS A crabby loose cannon because he had a bad cold and hadn't slept much the night before. James dropped him off with me just the same. After his lunch, he could barely keep his eyes open. I brushed the sand and crumbs from my bedroll and folded it in half so that it would be twice as comfortable for him. I covered him with my jacket and put my knit hat on his head. He liked that. I started to tell him a bedtime-story version of *Dog Day Afternoon*. He fell asleep in about two seconds. I didn't want to get sick, so I sat out on the front porch. I cracked open the copy of *Glengarry Glen Ross* Marie let me borrow. I got pretty deep into it when I heard Roy crying inside.

"Jesus Christ, Roy. What happened?" He was sitting upright, covered in diarrhea. It looked like he'd been sprayed with A1 sauce. The smell had a toxic chemical component to it not found in your everyday shit. He was freaked out because his hands were messy. He held them up for me. It was a damn good thing he couldn't see the rest of him. He was probably thinking, How the fuck did this shit get all over my hands while I was sleeping? Please clean them at once.

"Sorry, kid, but that's horrible." I couldn't hide my expression. Roy stopped crying on a dime and smiled, proud of himself. He clapped his hands, liberating a poisonous mist into the room. Then he raised one hand toward his runny nose.

"No, no, no. Don't do that." I grabbed his slippery wrist just in time. I scooped him up, then carried him—at arm's length—into the bathroom. "Dear God in heaven." He loved it.

I set him down on the floor and turned on the shower. There was no graceful way to free him from his soiled clothes so I just went for it. His head was further beshitted as it passed laboriously through the opening of his shirt. I started taking off all of my own clothes. Roy was curious. He reached up for my crotch. It shocked me.

"Get out of there," I laughed. "Jesus, kid. Didn't your old man teach you anything?"

He giggled, naked except for the shit.

I sat him in the middle of the tub. The water going down the drain turned *Psycho* brown. I sat like a bobsledder behind him and soaped us both up.

"Breathe in that good steam. It'll fix you right up." I demonstrated. He followed. He exploded with a series of yellow, ropy sneezes. I plucked the phlegm from his nose after each one and flung it at the drain. "Huh, kid? What I tell you? Better, right?"

I looked through the mommy bag for a change of clothes. There was a pair of green socks. That was it. "What the fuck, James?" Even though it hadn't happened yet on my watch, one had to think the possibility of a toddler shitting not just his pants but his entire outfit was not altogether far-fetched.

I'd been a little weirded out when Marie gave me that stack of Sidney's old clothes. But it was a good thing she did. I dressed Roy in a pair of black sweatpants, a black long-sleeved shirt, and a *Velvet Underground and Nico* T-shirt over that. He looked pale and exhausted, like a roadie for Soundgarden. I threw our dirty clothes and my makeshift bed into the washing machine. There was no detergent, so I ran it all through twice.

"Where'd he get those clothes?" James asked.

I told him everything.

"You just called Roy Sidney, you know."

"I did?"

"Yes. You said, 'Sidney had an accident.'"

"That's strange."

"Yes, it is. Do me a favor. Don't do that again. I'm superstitious. It's bad enough you got him in a dead kid's clothes."

THE NEXT TIME I worked for Marie I told her the whole story. I laid it on thick, making it sound like Roy's diarrhea was more explosive than it actually was. She liked the story, especially the parts about Sidney's clothes and me getting shat on.

"Babies and men and poop," she said. "Guys who don't have kids fear diaper changing almost as much as anything. That's the easy part."

"Really? Because it was not exactly a good time."

"That's because he was sick. He probably had the flu."

"Great. That means I'm going to get it. I'm fucked."

"Oh, don't be such a pussy."

I liked that Marie didn't have a problem using *pussy* as a playful put-down. She'd also drop a C-bomb in conversation now and then. "Well, anyway," I said, "it's a good thing you gave him those clothes."

Marie thought about it. "I think I'd like to see them on Roy. I don't know how it would make me feel, but I'm curious."

"Hang on," I said. "Don't you think the camera should be rolling when you say stuff like that?"

"Hmm."

"Would it be too fake if we let it roll and had that whole talk over?"

"I don't know. We can try."

"THAT'S A horrible expression," Jocelyn said. "I find it upsetting." She had her hands cupped around a full rocks glass. She was waiting for the ice in her Wild Turkey to melt to just the right size before drinking. It was after eight o'clock, but the front room at Nursing Holmes was orange with natural light. Some guys in a band were hauling their gear through the bar and into the bigger room.

"Can you just let the expression slide for the sake of the story?" Richie asked.

"It's not just the expression," Jocelyn said. "It's the whole story."

The other person at the table with us was a pretty Mexican kitchen worker named Milagro. The other Mexicans at Esposito's called her Flaca because they thought she was skinny. Flaca's English was broken. She backed Richie up. "What's wrong with saying 'piece of ass'?"

"You know what?" Jocelyn said. "There's nothing wrong with it. It's a fine expression. Succinct, and not wholly without texture. Use it liberally." She didn't feel like teaching Flaca both the English language and Feminism 101. She gave me a dirty look, which I shrugged off. Someone at a pool table in the next room executed an explosive break. Jocelyn flinched.

Richie continued where he left off. "For me it's a toss-up. I've had a few amazing 'wedding pieces.'"

I had drunk two beers and a shot. I was feeling all of them. "Hang on," I said. "For it to qualify as a wedding piece, do you have to fuck during the actual reception, or is it just someone you hook up with at a wedding and end up fucking?" I was a stickler for details.

Jocelyn blew smoke in all our faces.

"Either one," Richie said. "But let me go on record: It's way better if you screw during the festivities. It heightens it."

Flaca laughed, then said something in Spanish.

Richie continued. "I screwed a bridesmaid at my cousin Eleni's wedding. We were in a supply closet in the basement of the reception hall. I swear to God, Eleni and my uncle Nick were doing their father-daughter dance to 'All the Way' right above our heads. It was pretty priceless."

"Sounds classy," Jocelyn said.

"Hey, it wasn't my idea."

"Oh, in that case, sounds classy."

"What was her name?" I asked.

"Honestly? I could not tell you."

Jocelyn stood up. She frisbeed a Sam Adams beer coaster at the tabletop, and it skipped onto the battered red wool carpet. "In case you're all wondering," she said, "I'm going to the bathroom now to take a dump."

"Thanks for sharing," Richie said. We watched Jocelyn vanish, then Richie drew Flaca and me closer toward him. He smelled of Murray's pomade and Salems. He lowered his voice. "You ever get a wake piece?"

"Get the fuck out of here."

"What's a wake piece?" Flaca asked.

"You're telling me you got laid at a fucking wake?"

"Not at the wake. Right after. And it was someone I sort of knew back in high school."

"That's insane."

"Amy Dellorto," he reminisced. "You have to love a girl with the same last name as a carburetor."

"When the fuck was this?"

"I don't know. Couple years ago."

"Who died? Don't tell me it was her mother."

"No, our American history teacher, Mr. Savage. The only good teacher anyone in East Longmeadow ever had." Richie raised his glass, and we toasted this Mr. Savage.

"How in the fuck do you engineer something like that? What did you do, whisper in her ear while you were kneeling at the corpse?"

"A bunch of us met up for drinks afterward. She and I were catching up, and she says out of nowhere that she always liked me back then, but was too shy. We start making out in the bar. One thing led to another, blah, blah, blah, and you know that Budgetel on Route Five in Holyoke?"

"Wow."

"First floor. Third window from the right. I still look at it whenever I drive by."

"That's hilarious."

"The best part is, I was sitting on the edge of the bed with my Filene's Basement el cheapo suit pants pulled down to my ankles, and she's kneeling there, glazing my vase—"

"You just make that up, 'glazing my vase'?"

"I don't know. Maybe. Anyway, so she's glazing my vase, and the TV's on, and the *Happy Days* theme song starts playing. Not 'Rock Around the Clock,' the other one. I can't stop reading the names going by: Ron Howard, Henry Winkler, Donny Most, Anson Williams, blah, blah, blah. It was distracting, so I look down at my feet, and I'm wearing one brown sock and one blue sock."

"That is rich."

"A good time was had by all." He turned to Flaca. *"Tu comprendo?"*

Flaca nodded. Jocelyn was lingering at the jukebox. The Dream Syndicate's "Tell Me When It's Over" started playing. Richie leaned closer to Flacca and stroked her cheek with the back of his hand.

MARIE THOUGHT THE raw source material we'd taped so far seemed really good. And what wasn't could probably be fixed in editing. She said that's where the magic happened anyway. She mentioned something about the film *Burden of Dreams*. I was proud of myself for telling her I'd never seen it.

"You have to. It's a classic."

"Okay," I said. "I'll sniff it out when I have time."

"No you won't. I can tell." She popped the lens cap back onto the camera. "We're watching it now." She went to her room.

"What about work?" I called after her.

"This is work."

I followed her. "Okay, but you don't have to pay me for sitting around watching movies. I feel like I should be paying you."

She was getting the VCR ready. "Don't be ridiculous."

I sat in the armchair. Marie raced back to her bed and was lying down before the film's opening sequence. She patted the place next to her.

"You'll be able to see better from right here," she said.

"Okay." I was nervous. It didn't seem like she was coming on to me, but I could have counted on half a hand the number of times a girl inviting me to sit on her bed wasn't a come-on. I lay down next to her. I made sure there was a good foot of space between us.

"Are you okay with this?" she asked.

"Fine, why?"

"Just making sure."

Marie said *Burden of Dreams* was one of her favorite films. She'd seen it at least fifty times. She wasn't kidding.

She deconstructed and reassembled it as it went by. Usually that kind of running commentary would have driven me fucking crazy. But hers was insightful without making me feel like a fucking dope.

She grabbed my arm. "This part coming up is horrible."

"What happens?"

"Just watch." Ten seconds later some native day laborers hired to work on the film set were feared to have been crushed beneath an enormous portaged boat.

I groaned. "Do they die?"

"Watch."

I heard Marie start to sniffle as the scene played out on the screen. I looked at her out of the corner of my eye. "Are you okay?"

"I will be. It's still really hard for me to watch anything where people die."

"We don't have to watch it." I started to get up to turn off the VCR.

She stopped me. "No. I want to watch it."

"Why, if it makes you feel like shit?"

"Because a lot of things make me feel that way." She hit Pause on the remote. We faced each other. "If I want to keep living, I can't avoid feeling the pain."

"Jesus, that's pretty heavy."

"Well, what do you want me to say?"

"No. It's just—honest to God—the only time I've ever

heard someone say something like that and mean it was in the movies." Like Debra Winger in *Terms of Endearment* or the guy in *Brian's Song*.

"I don't know what to tell you."

"I've never been through anything as heavy as you have."

"No one close to you has ever died?"

"No."

"Well, they will."

"Unless I die first."

"That's your plan for dealing with grief?"

"No, but sometimes I think about certain people dying—like my parents or my sister—I can't imagine it. I'd definitely rather die first."

"You don't strike me as a selfish person, but that's pretty selfish."

"I know."

"You wouldn't want to die first. Trust me. You wouldn't want to put your mother through that. If the grief didn't kill her, the guilt might."

"Guilt? I'm not saying I'd want her to feel responsible for me dying."

"It's the guilt she'd feel for wanting to go on living after you."

"I never thought of that."

"I mean, I'm not distraught every fraction of every second of every minute, right?"

"And that makes you feel guilty?"

"Yes." She shifted on her elbow. "I'm not an idiot. I know that's why I drink as much as I do."

"Guilt?"

She nodded.

"That fucking sucks."

"Things aren't the way I planned, but what can you do, right?"

"How do you do it?"

"I just do."

"Man."

"You know that Eleanor Roosevelt quote?" Marie asked.

"No."

"The end of it is, 'You must do the thing you think you cannot do.' I say it to myself a lot." She repeated the quote.

"I mean—and I swear, I'm not trying to be an asshole—what's the payoff?"

"I don't think you're an asshole. Payoff for what, doing the things I think I can't?"

"Mmm."

"I get to live with some hope."

"That what, you'll be happy again?"

"No. I don't think that's an option. More like there'll be some kind of tolerable balance between the glimpses of happy moments and the rest of them."

"Right." I nodded. "And you'll get back to zero."

She nodded and smiled weakly. "That's the idea."

"It's kind of like that joke," I said. "The one with the guy who keeps whacking himself over the head with a hammer."

"And?"

"And his friend asks him why he's doing that, and he says, 'Because it feels so good when I stop.'"

She liked the joke. "It's sort of like that. I'm not the only one doing the hitting, but I'd take the relief just the same."

"Sometimes I think I'm the guy in the joke."

"Which? The inquisitive friend?"

"I wish."

"You ask me some pretty okay questions."

"Thanks, but I wasn't trying to."

She liked that. "You weren't trying to. That's really good. Thanks."

"Thanks for what, saying something funny?"

"Yes."

I WALKED HOME with another bag of Sidney's clothes. If Marie was thanking me for inadvertently saying something funny and cheering her up, I wondered how she'd react if I actually tried to do something nice for her. I got an idea. When I got home, I went through the bag of clothes and laid out Roy's outfit for the next day: a pair of cherry-red jeans and a mostly green hand-knit Icelandic sweater.

I hoped Marie liked it.

I got into bed. I started to jerk off, imagining what the rest of the night with Marie could have been like if *Burden of Dreams* hadn't brought her down so hard. I couldn't pull it off. It felt wrong. It had nothing to do with Jocelyn or exhaustion. I just couldn't get beyond the real image of Marie bummed out when those people in the movie got crushed by the boat.

I WAS WAITING on the front porch for them when James drove up with Roy.

"You're up early," James said.

"I have a big day ahead of me."

"You and me both." He thought about it. "What the fuck do you have to do?"

"Just the usual. Hang out with my best-buddy pal, Roy." He ran right at me.

"Jesus Christ," James said. "Did you shave?"

"Kind of. The razor was like a butter knife."

"Interesting." James was looking down his nose at my work.

I self-consciously stroked my cheeks. "You like it?"

"Yes," he said. "Very much. Now come on over here and suck my dick." He threw a playful backhand that I avoided.

"As much as I'd like to, I really can't." I tossed Roy up into the air and caught him. He started coughing.

"Hey, go easy on him. He's still not a hundred percent."

"You still feeling crummy, kid?" I held him with one

arm, like he was a full grocery bag. "You're looking pretty pink."

James watched us. "I guess it would be okay if you dropped me off and took the rig for the day."

"Nah, I figured we'd just poke around the neighborhood and entertain ourselves with the local flora and fauna."

"Flora and fauna? What the fuck's got into you?"

"How do you mean?"

"You're up early. You shaved. I swear to God, if your hair was combed, I'd shit blood right here on the lawn."

"Nothing has got into me. This is me feeling reasonably okay."

"I don't think I like it."

I STRIPPED ROY out of his outfit and dressed him in Sidney's clothes. "Honestly, kid, it's not the look for you, but it's a special occasion." Standing there in the pants and sweater, he looked like a psychedelic-era Clancy Brother. "I dig the red slacks, but the sweater's a bit much." Roy was scratching at his neck and wrists. "Want me to take that off you?" I tried to remove it, and he protested. "Okay. The sweater stays." I got him in his coat and Wellingtons, and we strolled toward the dead-end side of Opal Cove Road.

As we approached Marie's, I could hear a dog barking somewhere out of sight. It was too thin and yappy to be Tinker. Roy let out a small, fearful moan.

"Don't sweat it, kid. This time I'm prepared. Check this out." From beneath the stroller, I produced a sufficient length of copper pipe with an ugly, unfriendly T junction soldered to one end. "Like your old man says, you got to have the right tools to do the job." Roy wanted me to give him the pipe. "I can't, kid." He insisted, so I let him hold it. I felt less safe. "But if I spot Cujo"—I pointed at my chest—"the pipe goes to you know who."

We tried Marie's front door, but there was no answer. We went around to the back, and I banged on the storm door. I wanted to surprise her, so I kept Roy out of sight, off to the side. A light went on in the kitchen. Marie answered the door wearing a pink terry-cloth bathrobe. She didn't look too good. She was either hungover or had just gotten out of bed, or both.

"Hey," I said through the screen.

"I thought you couldn't work today."

"I can't."

She was confused. "Well, then . . ." She rubbed her eyes and scratched her head. "What are you doing here?"

"Did you just wake up?"

"Mmyeah, about three seconds ago."

"Sorry."

"I couldn't get to sleep, so I took a sleeping pill at around four."

"Oh, man. Should we leave?"

"Who's we?"

"Roy and me." I pulled Roy into view.

Marie perked right up. "No, you shouldn't go. You should come in." I carried Roy into the kitchen. "Hey there, Roy. It's good to see you again." Marie extended her hand for him to shake. He was cautious.

"It's okay, kid. Marie's our friend. Look." I shook her hand.

"Yeah, Roy, friends." She kissed me on the cheek.

"See," I said. "Marie is a friend."

"Can I give Roy a kiss?" Marie asked Roy. She leaned in and kissed him. He smiled. "Look at that smile. What beautiful teeth you have. Would you like a drink of milk?" Roy reached for the refrigerator. "You want something in the fridge?" Marie held out her arms for Roy to come to her. "Can I hold him?"

"If he'll let you, be my guest." I passed Roy to Marie, and he went without a fight. She wore him on her hip and went to the fridge.

"Let's see what we have in here for you, Roy." They disappeared behind the open door. Light poured out onto the beige linoleum. Roy made a noise like he was struggling to reach something. "What is it?" Marie asked. "You want ketchup? No? An egg?" That was it. "Oh, Roy wants an egg." Marie's head appeared over the door. "Can Roy have an egg?"

"I don't see why not."

"That's great news, Roy. Let's get you out of your coat and boots, and Marie will make you an egg, okay?" She set Roy on the floor and unbuttoned his coat. She gasped when she saw Sidney's sweater on him. She put her hand on her mouth, then stood up so that she could take all of him in.

"Oh, my God. And the pants, too." She started to cry.

I felt like a heel. "I thought you wanted to see them on him," I said. I tried to close Roy's coat. Marie stopped me.

"No, don't," she said. "I do want to see them. It's just a shock." She picked Roy up and squeezed him. She ran her hands over the sweater and pants.

"You sure?"

"Yes." She smiled at me, then kissed Roy's face. She pressed his head against her chest and rested her chin on the top of his head. "Thank you," she said. "Both of you."

Roy ate his scrambled egg with ketchup and toast off a green plastic plate decorated with an action scene from the Teenage Mutant Ninja Turtles comics. Marie and I split an omelet with blue cheese and tomato. We sat at her small kitchen table.

"It's nice not to be eating in a restaurant," I said.

Marie gave my coffee a warmer. "Not much of a cook?"

"I'd like to be, but I never found the time." Never found time? I didn't really know the reason why I'd never learned to cook, but it sure as fuck wasn't because of a lack of time.

"I was a pretty okay cook," Marie said. "I just haven't felt like it."

I impaled a chunk of omelet with my fork and raised it. "I'd say you're still a pretty okay cook."

"It's just an omelet."

"Well, it's a good one."

"Thanks. Watching someone enjoy is half the fun of cooking."

"FYI, I'm enjoying this." I chewed and watched her watch me. "Is it still fun?"

She smiled. "It's not bad."

I turned to Roy. "What about you? You having fun, Roy? His Roy-al Highness? Little Lord Fauntle-Roy?" I messed up his hair.

"You should never disturb a man when he's eating," Marie said.

"So true." We watched him eat.

"Have you ever had an aged sirloin?" Marie asked. "I mean, a really good, really well prepared aged sirloin?"

"I might have."

"No, no, if you had one, you'd know." She closed her eyes and bit her lower lip.

"Then I guess I haven't."

"It's been a while for me. What if I cooked one?"

"Now?"

"Not now. For dinner."

I could feel my face get hotter. "Well . . . sure. That would be awesome."

"There's a great butcher in Yarmouth." She used her napkin to wipe the ketchup from around Roy's mouth.

"That seems like a lot of trouble."

"We could all go?"

"What do you think, Roy? You have any plans for the day?"

Marie tried to wipe his face again, but he wasn't into it. "I think the ketchup's giving him a little contact rash." She touched the corresponding area around her own mouth. "See? Right here?"

MARIE SAID ROY and I should play in Sidney's room while she got dressed.

"This is where I work when I'm not taking care of you. Pretty cool, huh?" Roy was momentarily paralyzed by the sheer number of things before him. When he got his bearings, he went straight for the movie camera. I intercepted him. "Sorry, kid. This is the one thing you can't touch. This is Marie's movie camera." He looked at me like a puzzled dog. "Cam-er-a," I repeated loud and clear. "Can you say cam-er-a?"

Marie called from her bedroom. "Why don't you shoot a little of him?"

"For what?"

"I don't know. He might find it interesting."

"Would you like that, Roy? You want me to take your picture?" It was the first time since I'd started taking care of him that I thought he knew exactly what the fuck

I was talking about. He started giggling and shaking like a crazy motherfucker. It was pretty great to see. "Okay. Okay." I was laughing. "Just give me two seconds."

I fired up the camera and looked through the view-finder. Marie's empty chair came into sharp focus. I collected Roy and sat him in it. I got back behind the camera. Roy looked like a tiny black-and-white photocopy of himself. I started recording.

"Okay, Roy, here's your big break. What would you like to say to the people?" I stuck an invisible microphone in front of his face. Roy kicked his legs and shrieked with delight. It was hilarious.

Marie appeared in the doorway. "What are you two clowns up to in here?"

"I HONESTLY DIDN'T THINK I'd ever be doing this again," Marie said as we installed Sidney's old car seat in her Subaru.

I pulled on one of the fastening straps until it was taut. "You think this is tight enough?" She jerked on it and nodded. I hoisted Roy and we strapped him in.

"You feel like driving?" Marie asked, wearing the key ring on her index finger.

"Really?" My voice cracked.

"Are you old enough?" She handed off the keys to me as we passed each other around the back of the car. I got in. Marie settled into the passenger seat. "Feel free to adjust anything if you're cramped." I fixed my grip at ten and two. The worn leather cover around the steering wheel was sticky.

"Actually, it all feels pretty good."

The last time Marie had driven, she killed the engine without first turning off the tape player. When I started the car, the song "Rolling Moon" by the Chills played mid-song. "Oh, fantastic choice," I said. "I love the Chills."

Marie turned the music off, then said, "Me, too, but do you mind if we don't listen to this right now? They can be a little depressing."

"No problem. Quiet's good. So where are we going exactly."

"Well, it's basically a straight shot once you get back onto Twenty-eight. When we get into Yarmouth—right around the center of town—I'll tell you which way to go." I was a slightly less nervous driver than I was a passenger. I needed to hear the simplest of directions—even to places I'd been before—four or five times. I knew it didn't make any sense, but I couldn't help myself.

"Back up a second," I said. "Which direction do I go on Twenty-eight?"

Marie had some fun with me. "Is this your first trip to Cape Cod?"

"I'm not even going to dignify that with an answer."

"Okay. Let me rephrase the question. Is Yarmouth anywhere between East Falmouth and Boston?"

I smiled without looking at her. "No, I do not believe it is."

"So, Professor, seeing as Boston is east of where we are right now, which direction do we go on Twenty-eight to get to Yarmouth?"

I looked back at Roy. "Are you catching what she's doing up here, kid? I mean, do I deserve this kind of abuse?"

"Seems to me you'd be better off asking him which direction we go on Twenty-eight."

"That's it. I've taken all I'm going to take." I opened the door and pretended to be getting out of the car. "I'm outta here and I'm never coming back."

Roy started to cry. Marie turned in her seat. "It's okay, Roy. He was just playing." She grabbed my arm. "Tell him you're not going anywhere."

"I'm not going anywhere. Look. I'm still here. We're all going to the store—together. Me. You. Marie." I closed the door and buckled my seat belt for effect. Roy stopped crying, but his lip was still quivering.

"He was just pretending, Roy." Marie and I looked at each other. She reached back and took hold of one of Roy's feet. She gave it a playful wiggle, and he smiled.

"What can I say?" I asked her quietly. "I guess the kid really likes me."

"I think it's more like love."

"Crazy, huh?"

"Not so much." We had to turn away from each other to keep from cracking up. We didn't want Roy to think we were laughing at him.

．　．　．

AFTER JAMES picked up Roy, I biked down to Spunt's for some laundry detergent. Ricky was glad to see me. While I comparison-shopped, he told me about how Bob Lobel, the legendary Boston sportscaster, had gassed up there yesterday on his way out to Truro.

"No shit."

"Uh-huh."

"Was he a nice guy?"

"He was awesome."

"That's cool. I always liked Bob Lobel. It would be a drag if he turned out to be a dick in real life."

"No, not Bob Lobel. Look." He held up a disposable camera. "There's four pictures of me and him. I took them myself." It was nice to see how proud Ricky was of the whole thing.

"That's really cool."

"Only twenty more pictures to go."

"I hope you get some good ones."

"Me too. Can I take one of you?"

I was surprised. "You want a photo of me?"

"I won't use the flash if it bothers your eyes. Some people get those little things when they look at a flash." He wiggled his fingers in the air.

"Jesus, Ricky. It's not the flash."

"Awesome, 'cause I think it'll come out better with

it." He raised the camera to his face. "Stay right there." I froze. "Smile."

"I am smiling."

He snapped the photo. "One more, just in case." He snapped another. "How about one with me and you in it?"

"Sure, why not?"

"But stand right here so it's like the ones with me and Bob Lobel." Ricky leaned his head in over the middle of the counter. I did the same. We were almost cheek to cheek. He snapped two photos.

"Awesome. Only sixteen more pictures to go."

I joked with him. "You could take a hundred pictures. None of them are going to come out as good as the ones of me."

He giggled. "That's a good one." He started to ring up the detergent. "Doing laundry, Pay Phone?"

I felt like joking some more with him. "What, this? No. I use it instead of shampoo."

"For serious?"

"Hell yeah."

"Whoa." He ran his fingers through his hair, trying to imagine what it would feel like shampooed with Tide. "I never heard of anybody doing that before."

"Sure you have. Everybody knows All-Tempa-Cheer is gentlest on your scalp."

"It is?"

"Yeah, but you guys are out. This will do me fine." I started peeling dollar bills from a roll.

"You sure?" He craned his neck to see into the right aisle. "I thought we had that kind."

"Forget it. It's no biggie."

"If you watch the register, I'll go out back and see if we have some."

"No, don't bother."

"It's no bother. I want to."

"Don't." I started to feel like an asshole. I didn't think he was going to swallow the hook so completely and feel bad about disappointing me.

He came around the counter. "It's no bother, honest. It's my job."

"Really, Ricky," I grabbed him by the arm. "Don't." I think I scared him.

"Why?"

I loosened my grip. "Just don't, okay?"

EVEN AFTER WORKING in a restaurant for nearly three years, I knew just enough about wine to fuck up an eighty-dollar piece of meat. So I brought a fifth of Jack Daniel's to Marie's. Bourbon and beef. That's how they did it on *The Big Valley* and *The High Chaparral*.

Marie answered the back door wearing a white apron over her clothes. It was a cartoonish map of Italy with, *Sì, sono della Calabria!* splashed across it. Marie had eye shadow on. She kissed me on the cheek. Roy wasn't with me this time.

"Huh, Jack Daniel's." She examined the label. "I approve."

"It's downright upright," I said, quoting Frank Gifford from the Harveys Bristol Cream ad.

She was impressed. "You remember that commercial?"

"Please."

"What about this one?" She started singing, " 'Martini and Rossi on the rocks. Say yeh-eh-ess.' "

I finished the jingle in a sultry voice: "Yeeehhhsss."

LALO SCHIFRIN's made-for-TV music jiggled from a boom box on her kitchen counter.

"I love Lalo Schifrin," I said.

"Same here." She poured us both a glass of dark red wine. "Him and Ennio Morricone."

"Do not even get me started on how good Morricone is. We could be here all night."

I felt pretty comfortable, sitting at the table and watching the back of her as she prepped the steak at the stove. I always thought those gaucho pants made grown women look silly, but the jury was still out on whether Marie was pulling them off. As she shifted her weight, I could see the musculature of her peasant calves at work beneath her animated skin. More inky pinks and greens popped in contrast to her white, plunging-back angora sweater.

The grill pan objected with a prolonged hiss when the meat came into contact with it.

"What about the scene in *Raging Bull*," I asked. "Where whosie-whatsie there—La Motta's wife—is cooking him the steak?"

She turned a cheek to me. "You know, I actually started to hate De Niro in that scene—not as an actor, as a person."

"Really?"

"It's like, he was such a phenomenally good abusive asshole of a husband, there's no way he could have been acting."

"Then you must love it when he asks Joe Pesci if he fucked his wife?"

Marie came at me. I was startled. She raised a long, two-tined fork to my throat. "Did you fuck my wife? Why did you fuck my wife?"

THE STEAK WAS divided into two slabs, and Marie put the slightly more imposing one my plate. The blood rushed around my scalloped potatoes and stained their edges pink. Both of us were starving. We ate like marooned sailors.

"You were right," I said, talking around a tobacco plug of meat tucked into my cheek.

"Mmm." Marie was consumed by the pleasure of consuming.

"If I ever had an aged sirloin before, I would have known it."

"Mmm," she agreed.

"How do they get it so tender?"

She took a cleansing gulp of wine. "Decomposition."

"Oh, man, that's sick." I set my utensils down loudly.

Marie was amused, like the tribal elder who tells the Western traveler he's eating jellied goat testicles. "Don't think about it."

"Oh, okay," I sulked. "I'll try." I poached a piece of meat from her plate.

"Hey," she protested. "You purloined my loin."

"I did no such thing, Your Honor."

She looked at my plate. I hadn't touched my asparagus. "What, my vegetables aren't good enough for you?"

I selectively ate asparagus after Jocelyn said it made more than just my piss smell funny. "I just didn't want to fill up on it. Look." I took a bite.

"Well, I love it." Marie held a lemon-zested stalk in her fingers and powered through it like a gopher. The theme to *The Streets of San Francisco* came on. Marie pointed to the boom box. "Mmm," she said as she chewed. "Karl Malden. Criminally overlooked actor."

I SAT WAY BACK in my chair and put my hands on my stomach. "Good thing I didn't wear a belt."

"You and me both." She stood up so I could see. "I popped my top button as a precaution." I caught a small

Joe Pernice

shimmering triangle of electric blue before she sealed her pants up and sat back down. I pretended not to notice by raising a hand to my heart like I felt a massive coronary coming on. I was going to be funny and ask Marie if she knew CPR, but luckily I didn't. I had a flash of her screaming while paramedics tried to save her son. "But," she said, "I'm not too stuffed to sip some bourbon."

"You read my mind."

I watched as she reached up into the cabinet for two glasses.

"You a fan of car racing?" I asked.

"No," she said, intrigued by the question. "Why?"

"The checkered flag on your shoulder blade." I could just make out a leading corner of it poking out from under her sweater.

"That's not a flag. It's a kerchief." She got in front of my chair with her back to me. "Look." Like a wife whose dress is about to be zipped by her husband, she bent her neck forward and lifted her hair out of the way. I drew back the fuzzy neckline of her sweater.

"Whoa. That's definitely not a checkered flag."

"No," she laughed. "It isn't. You like it?"

"Is it wrong if I say I do?"

"I think it would be wrong if you said you didn't."

"Then I like it."

It was a full-body profile of a kneeling, naked pinup girl. Something slightly more X-rated than what you might see painted on a World War II fighter plane. The checkerboard kerchief in her blond hair gave the impression that she was a good all-American girl who enjoyed a good all-American screwing after a secluded picnic lunch.

"I have her twin on the other side." Marie reached over her opposite shoulder and guided me to the spot. She left her hand on mine. My heart started pounding. She pulled my hand around her and parked it on her right breast. "Is this okay?" she asked. We were both stone-cold sober.

"I think so." My left hand found her other breast. I automatically handled her the way Jocelyn liked to be handled. I kissed her exposed back. She started to laugh. "Should I stop?" I asked.

"No, please don't. Just do everything a bit harder."

I did. She started grinding her ass against me. I grabbed her by the hip bones and pulled.

"Tell me one thing," she said between breaths.

"Mmm," I said with my mouth against her back.

"And I want the truth."

"Mmm."

"Did you really not fuck me last time?"

"No," I said.

"I think this time you should."

AFTERWARD WE LAY on our backs in the dark without talking. I felt surprisingly okay about the whole thing, except for not knowing what Marie was thinking.

I cleared my throat just to let her know I was still there. I tapped a galloping, four-fingered beat on the mattress that would have driven Jocelyn nuts. Marie didn't make a peep. Her silence grew too uncomfortably big to ignore.

"Are you freaked out?" I finally asked. She didn't answer. "You are, aren't you?"

"Hmm?"

I sat up. "Are you asleep?" I asked at louder-than-bedroom volume.

"Was."

"Jesus."

"Sorry."

I laughed. "Don't be sorry."

"So tired."

"Do you always zonk out after sex . . . like a guy?"

She let out a short, closemouthed laugh. "You offended?" She would rather have been sleeping. I knew that feeling.

"God, no." My tone was unmistakably revelatory.

She stroked my shin once with her foot, then shifted into the fetal position. Her knees were touching my thigh.

"You weren't talking," I said. "I figured . . ."

"You, either."

I thought about that for a bit. "I wasn't, was I?"

She didn't answer. I let her go. Within seconds, her breathing was even and automatic.

I WOKE UP in the middle of the night without the terrifying sensation of not knowing where I was. Woke without lying perfectly still for fear of falling from the Empire State Building; without the anxiety of having strolled into a classroom after months of truancy, only to learn the final exam was that day; without thinking all of my teeth had just mysteriously fallen out.

I did wake with the very real sensation of having to take a massive shit. I could tell it was going to be an embarrassing, conspicuous, and hostile parting. Marie was still curled up, but facing the other way. I decided to get dressed and split back to my sister's. Then I thought that would be a ridiculous thing to do. Marie's Eleanor Roosevelt quote went through my head.

Fuck it. I tiptoed naked to the kitchen, found my cigarettes, then—as quietly as I could—destroyed her bathroom.

On my way back to the bedroom, I stopped at Sidney's open door. My eyes skipped over the dark, kaleidoscopic clutter of his room, and rested on two moons beyond the sliding glass doors: One glowed still. The other was indiscriminately pulled apart and put back together by the undulating surface of Opal Cove.

I took a few steps into the room, but stopped abruptly when I kicked a small toy that lit up in flashing red and played that tune about the kids on the bus going up and down all through the town. I managed to shut the fucking thing off by the third or fourth refrain. I carefully put the toy down and got out of Sidney's room.

I sneaked back into Marie's bed. She'd slept through it all, including the multiple flushes. She only partially woke when I started laughing softly.

"'t's so funny?"

"*Shhh.*" I patted her ass. "Keep sleeping."

I WAS DREAMING about James and Roy and me at Spunt's. James had just finished filling Roy's sippy cup—which was about five times as big as it is in real life—with hot coffee.

"Everybody knows coffee's good for kids," James said.

"I've never heard of that."

"Sure you have," James said. "Plus, he loves it."

"You're out of your mind."

"No I'm not. Watch."

"Dude, he's going to fucking scald himself." I tried to swat the cup away, but James grabbed my arm and stopped me. I woke up before Roy took a sip.

Marie wasn't in bed. Sunlight broke into the room between the partially drawn curtains. An otherwise welcoming aroma of coffee was burned around the edges, like the Mr. Coffee had been on for some time. The kitchen faucet went on, then off. I got up and put my clothes on. If Marie heard me, she didn't say anything.

Her elbows were on the kitchen table. She was

enveloped by the pink terry-cloth bathrobe. Her face was in her hands. I wishful-thought that maybe she was just tired, but I knew nobody *that* tired gets out of bed unless they absolutely have to. I put my hand on her shoulder. She wasn't startled. She dropped her hands to her lap.

"Hey," I said.

"Hey." She didn't try to hide the fact that she'd been crying.

"What is it?"

She just shook her head and said, "I can't."

"Can't what?"

"I can't do this. I'm sorry. I just can't."

I fell into one of the chairs. Her dirty utensils and napkin from the night before were in front of me. "You can't?"

"No."

I lit a cigarette and listened to the elliptical hum of the refrigerator's compressor motor. "What about——"

"Don't," she said.

I threw a nod in the direction of her bedroom. "And all that was just——"

"Please, don't. I'm asking you, please." She looked like she was begging me to spare her life. Maybe she was.

I pretended to shrug the whole thing off. "It's no big deal."

She could tell I was stung pretty bad, but she also knew how to accept a gift. "Thank you."

I just sat there for a little while, staring at a framed needlepoint primer hanging on the wall. It said, I Am

Joe Pernice

the Queen of the Kitchen. All Those Who Do Not Bow Down to Me Can STARVE.

"It's because I plugged your toilet, isn't it?"

She came right back at me, weepy and laughing at the same time. "I thought I was the one who plugged it."

I smiled, but couldn't go on with the flirty repartee. "And what about the movie?" I asked.

"I was hoping you'd still want to."

"Sure."

She reached across the table for my hand. I let her have it, but I thought I was going to come apart. I stood up abruptly. "I'm going to go now."

Marie tightened her grip on my hand. I turned my head away. She gave my arm an attention-getting tug. "Let me see you first." I didn't want to, but I faced her. She let me go only after I faked a smile.

I pulled Sweet Thunder out from under her back porch. Through the walls of the house, I could hear her crying for a number of things—the least of which was me.

JAMES AND DOGSHIT were sitting on the hood of the Suburban. James stood when he saw me. He semaphored me in like I would have otherwise biked right by him— which is exactly what I felt like doing. "What do you want first," he asked me. "The good news or the bad news?"

"I don't fucking care."

"What crawled up your ass?"

"Nothing."

"Fine. The good news is, you don't have to watch Roy anymore."

"That's the good news?"

"The bad news is, she knows."

"Who knows what?"

"Pamela. She knows about you watching Roy."

"Come again?"

"She knows you've been—"

I came uncorked. "What the fuck do you mean she knows?"

James got defensive. "Hey, listen, pal. You're the one who dressed him in that crazy fucking outfit."

"Yeah, I did. But you were supposed to change him out of it before you brought him home."

"Well, I didn't. And now she knows. So sue me."

"Fuck me," I said. "Motherfuck me."

Dogshit chimed in. "How'd she figure out just from seeing Roy in the clothes that he'd been watching him?"

"Shut the fuck up."

"Yes, James," I said sarcastically. "How did she put two and two together? What, did Roy learn how to fucking talk overnight, you moron?"

"Hey, back off, Jack."

I couldn't back off. "You know, when Pamela's your ex-wife, she'll still be my sister, you fucking idiot."

"Whoa, dude." Dogshit put his hand on my shoulder. "Chill out."

I swatted his hand off me. "I'm not going to chill out."

"Oooh-kay," Dogshit said. "I think I'll take a little walk and let you guys—"

"Don't fucking bother," James said. "We're not going to be here that long."

"What are you going to do, level me with one punch?"

"Is that what you want?" James yelled. He took a step toward me. "Is that what you fucking want?"

Dogshit got in front of him. "No. It's definitely not what he wants."

"Then somebody should stuff a fucking sock in it," James said.

"That sounds like a great idea," Dogshit said. "Dude," he appealed to me.

"You know, James, you're a real pisser. I lie to her fucking face. My sister. For you. Fuck knows what shit things you did to make her want to divorce you, but no matter. I lied to her anyway. I could have fucked you over a few times but I didn't. I just lied to her like a genuine fucking asshole. For you. Not me. You."

"You think I don't know that? You think I don't fucking know that?"

I was exasperated and worn down. "Well, if you knew it, why'd you tell her? I mean, couldn't you have lied to her just one more time? You had to know she was going to be completely bullshit with me. What were you thinking? Jesus."

"What do you want me to say? I'm sorry? Is that what you want me to say?"

"Dude," Dogshit said to me. "Is that all you want?"

"I don't fucking know what I want. I swear to God, I don't."

Dogshit turned to James. "I think that's all he wants."

"Fine," James said. "I'm sorry. I am."

I knew what was at risk when I agreed to be party to James's plan, but I needed to be mad at somebody. He held out his hand for me to shake, but I wouldn't take it. "Whatever," I said. I pointed Sweet Thunder toward Plymouth Street and started pedaling. I added my sister Pamela to the short list of women I'd forced out of my life.

"Oh, that's right. Whatever," James called after me. "I apologized. I'm not going to fucking beg you to accept."

I BIKED STRAIGHT to the phone booth at Spunt's and dialed Jocelyn's number. No answer, no machine, nothing.

"Fuck! Fuck! Fuck! Fuck! Fuck!"

I whacked a glass panel with the receiver, but not hard enough to break anything. I tried to slam the phone-booth door, but it was designed so that no matter how much force you put into it, it always closes nice and easy. I had to go back to New York and look for Jocelyn. Ricky was watching me from inside the store. He gave me a small, concerned wave. I left the Spunt's parking lot and pedaled away from East Falmouth. Fuck Tommy the cop. If he—or any other cop—picked me up, all the better. I'd give him my word never to return so long as he got me off Cape Cod ASAP. I took the feeder ramp onto Route 28 and knowingly became a criminal.

AS I ASCENDED the back stairs, I could hear Richie on the porch, talking to someone on the phone. "I'm going to have to call you back," he said excitedly when he saw me. He was wearing nothing but a raunchy lime-green towel around his waist. The towel was so small that if the temperature outside had been five to ten degrees higher, his nut sack would have swung visibly—like a produce bag containing two kiwis. "Dude," he said, "you are not going to fucking believe this."

"What?"

"This." He handed me an envelope.

"What's this, a summons?"

"Kind of."

I checked out the return address. "From Sub Pop?"

"No shit, it is. Read it." I peeked into the envelope like it could have been from the Unabomber. "Out loud," Richie added. "I want to hear someone else say the words. And make sure you enunciate."

"'Dear Losers: This letter concerns your crummy demo tape. While it leaves much to be desired, miraculously, it isn't as ear-piercingly horrible as the other thousand we received that day. One song in particular, "Black

Smoke, No Pope," does not completely suck. Though we can't—for legal reasons—encourage you to continue making music, this letter is intended to come infinitely close to that point. Sincerely, Sub Pop Records.'

"What the fuck is this?"

Richie was smiling. "Dude, it's positive reinforcement."

"Get the fuck out of here."

"It is. I'm serious. They like our tape." He tried to high-five me.

"Where in this letter does it say that?"

"Right here. We're not as ear-piercingly horrible as everyone else. We don't completely suck."

"That's them liking it?"

"Hello, come-guzzler, it's Sub Pop we're talking about here. Maybe you've heard of them? Nirvana? Sebadoh? Mudhoney? Beat Happening—"

"Yes, I'm well aware of who is on the label, thank you. But this doesn't sound like they're into it."

"Dude, that's their way. Trust me. Think about the Clash. Think about the Pistols. What did the audience do when they liked them? They covered them with loogies."

"That's different."

"It isn't."

"I don't know."

"I do. Sub Pop is going to fucking sign the Young Accuser." He started dancing around, and his towel fell to the porch floor. He made no move to cover himself.

"Dude, wrap that shit up." He boosted himself up onto the railing and yelled, "Sub Pop is going to sign the Young Accuser. Mark my words."

"You're fucking insane."

"And you are afraid of success."

"Oh, I am?"

"That's okay, though, because I'm not. You can be the shy, moody one in the band. Just grab on to this little old belt loop and hang on tight. We're going places."

"I'm not grabbing on to anything. Would you put some fucking clothes on."

Richie wasn't listening. "Okay, what we do is we start four-tracking our asses off. Eight days a week. Morning, noon, and night. None of this 'I don't really feel like it right now' bullshit. And we get salty. We get tight. But not too tight. We don't want to turn into fucking Timbuk Three." He had a revelation. "I got it. Maybe we ask Melanie to play with us. Nothing too over-the-top. Just a kick and snare. Dyke drummers go over huge in Seattle. I'm serious. They eat that shit up."

"At least put your towel back on."

Richie went on with rattling off his plans. They were like cracks in the ice spoking out from a single point of impact.

I read the letter a few more times to myself. I wished it had been even more discouraging. I didn't know how to tell him I was moving to Brooklyn as soon as I could find someone to take my room.

DONNELLY'S PARKING LOT was empty. My hands were shaking as I fed change into the Coke machine right outside the front door. I shielded my bad molar with my tongue and drained most of the icy soda in the first go. I inhaled my cigarette like a POW upon liberation. God-damnit, it felt good as the caffeine and nicotine exerted their influence.

I heard someone riding a go-kart out back. The driver knew the track like the back of his hand. He stepped on and off the gas pedal in a regular, predictable sequence. I closed my eyes and imagined it was me—younger and unspoiled—tooling around and around the track. I moved Sweet Thunder's handlebars like I was steering the kart. I might even have been making audible, muffled motor sounds. In my mind I know I was.

"Do you need help, son?"

I opened my eyes, startled. Mr. Donnelly Jr. was standing close enough to touch me. "No."

"You sure about that?"

"You scared me." I could still hear the sole kart going at it out back.

"You looked like you were going to have a seizure."

I laughed it off. "No."

"That's good." He waited a couple beats. "Well, what were you doing?"

I didn't feel like lying. "I was listening."

"To the engine?"

"Yes." That didn't seem so strange to him. "And imagining myself behind the wheel."

He chuckled. "Why pretend?"

"I wasn't exactly pretending."

He patted me on the back. "Why not come and try it for real."

"That's okay."

"Come on. I won't even charge you."

"Thanks, but I think I'd rather just think about it."

"You would?"

"I think so."

"Okay. Suit yourself." He was shaking his head. Once again, he did not know what the fuck to make of me. "Suit yourself." He opened the door to his known quantity and disappeared into it.

I LOOKED OUT Jocelyn's front window. A maroon Lincoln Town Car was parked on the opposite side of Sixth Avenue. The driver was leaning against the outside of the door, reading a paper.

"Our car's here," I said. Jocelyn was buzzing around the apartment in her underwear, stuffing clothes and toiletries into a backpack. "You go down. I just need a couple minutes." She gave me a peck, then took my face in her hands, looked it over, and planted a longer kiss, into which I fell. She pulled herself away from me. "Do you have everything?"

"Yes," I said, mildly annoyed.

"Passport? License? Birth certificate?"

"Yes. Yes. Yes."

"Just checking. I don't want this to fall apart at the eleventh hour."

"It won't."

She straightened my tie beneath my denim jacket. "I like the Sam Shepard thing you have going on. You look handsome."

"You too." I touched the front clasp of her white bra and ran my finger down her stomach. She sucked it in out of reach before I could go too far.

"Later," she protested playfully.

"Now."

"Don't be greedy. We're going to have each other for the rest of our lives." She bounded off to the bathroom. She looked like she was crossing a river by stepping on the heads of crocodiles. "Now go, or we'll lose the car." I looked out the window. The Lincoln was still there. I was closing the apartment door behind me when I heard Jocelyn call out like a Hollywood cowgirl, "Oh, yoo-hoo? Yoooo-hoooo?" I poked my head around the door to see Jocelyn poking her head around the bathroom door. We were two heads.

"What?" I asked.

"Are you still here?"

"No. I am not."

"Good." She was all smiles. I might have been, too.

I MADE IT about a mile, a mile and a half, back toward East Falmouth, when a cop car coming in the opposite direction flashed me. I stopped on the sandy shoulder and watched him pull a U-turn. He parked in front of me and got out of the cruiser. He stared at me. I stared right back at him. Neither one of us wanted to be the first to laugh.

Thanks to:

The Pernice family; the Stein family; Megan Lynch, Sarah Bowlin, and everyone else at Riverhead Books; Joyce Linehan; Marian Hebb at Hebb, Scheffer and Associates; Chris Parris-Lamb at the Gernert Company; Nicola Spunt; Jill Holmberg; Lou Barlow; Ken Harrington; Neal J. Huff; Dr. Gordon Yanchyshyn; John Niven; David Barker; Adam Pettle; Jo Ann Wasserman; V. Paul Coyne; Benjamin Wheelock; Richard Bonanno; Peyton Pinkerton (Connecticut is actually the state in *his* way); Bob Pernice; James Walbourne; Patrick Berkery; Thom Monahan; Jose Ayerve; Ric Menck; Michael Belitsky; Joe Harvard; and Michael Deming.

Most of all, thanks to my wife and son for their unending love and for daring me daily.